DATE DUE			

The Revelation of Saint Bruce

The Revelation of
SAINT BRUCE

TRES SEYMOUR

ORCHARD BOOKS
New York

Note: The Bible passages that appear throughout this book are from the King James Version.

Orchard Books, 95 Madison Avenue, New York, NY 10016

Manufactured in the United States of America
Book design by Mina Greenstein
The text of this book is set in 12 point Goudy Old Style.
10   9   8   7   6   5   4   3   2   1

Library of Congress Cataloging-in-Publication Data
Seymour, Tres.
The revelation of Saint Bruce / by Tres Seymour.
    p.   cm.
Summary: When high-school senior Bruce Wells inadvertently snitches on his friends, he learns painful lessons about being true to himself and different from his classmates.
ISBN 0-531-30109-5 (trade : alk. paper). —
ISBN 0-531-33109-1 (lib. bdg. : alk. paper)
[1. Individuality—Fiction. 2. Interpersonal relations—Fiction. 3. Friendship—Fiction. 4. High schools—Fiction. 5. Conduct of life—Fiction. 6. Schools—Fiction.]   I. Title.
PZ7.S5253Re   1998   [Fic]—dc21   98-13719

For Mitch

part ONE

My *best friend,* for my sins, is Jack LaRue. If you hang around Jack long enough, you will do immoral things.

Take, for example, the night we were at the pay phone across the street from Hardee's. Jack was calling home to explain to his dad why he would be late getting back from the movie.

"What are you going to tell him?" I asked.

"Flat tire," he said.

I was dubious. "You were supposed to be home an hour and a half ago. How long does it take to change a tire?"

"What am I supposed to tell him?" Jack said. "The truth? He'd crap a brick."

"What's so terrible about playing cards for an hour at Carrie's house?"

"My dad doesn't like her dad. Anyway, Bruce, what are you going to tell your folks?"

"The truth. I've never gotten away with a lie in my life. Reality is too full of details to try to cover all your tracks. It's always made me honest."

"It's always made you a weenie," Jack said. "*I've* never had any trouble. I figure you should never let anything get in the way of what you want to do." He slipped his quarter into the slot and dialed. Jack's dad answered; I could hear him shouting through the receiver.

"Sorry, Dad," Jack said, "I'll be home in just a minute. There were these guys in a pickup, see, and they passed us on a double yellow line and threw a pop bottle out the window. I ran over it and blew a tire and it's taken us forever to get it fixed. Yeah? Okay, I'll drive carefully. Yeah. Bye." He hung up. "No sweat," he said.

"You're disgusting. That excuse would have made a cat laugh. I would never have gotten away with that. Dad would have wanted to see the tires."

Jack started out of the booth, but the pay phone made a strange grinding sound followed by a chinkle, and Jack stuck his finger in the coin return. He fished out a quarter, then another, then another, one after the next. He started stuffing them in his pockets.

"What do you think you're doing?"

"Man! You don't get this lucky every day! It's a Jack-pot!" He pointed at his own chest.

"You are robbing the phone company."

"At a quarter a call, they rob us every time we pick up the receiver."

"Come on, Jack. Put them back."

"No way! There must be ten dollars here!"

I shifted and glanced around—any moment now a policeman would no doubt arrive and I would have to call Mom and Dad from jail and explain that Jack and I were nabbed during a phone-booth heist. I felt like I ought to stop Jack somehow. I *should* have. But I didn't.

He jogged his jeans up and down to settle the money in them, and we walked away.

Jack gave the incident no more thought. He's gifted with an easy conscience. I, on the other hand, stewed. It kept nagging at me that he shouldn't have done it, shouldn't have done it, shouldn't have done it. The perfect order of the universe was fraying at the seams, and Jack LaRue was picking at the loose threads. (I have a lot of these—what my sister Lee Ann calls my "deep and stupid thoughts.")

But I couldn't help it. It was a compulsion. And when Jack suddenly announced, when he and I and our friends Carrie, Ellis, and Theresa were having a slice of pizza, that he was footing the bill for dinner, I couldn't help myself then either.

"I'll pay for my own, Jack," I said.

Carrie looked at me across the table. Her avowed goal is to join Mensa, a kind of club for geniuses. She is always delighted to share the fact that her IQ is 155. She keeps her hair pulled back, which always makes her look studious and severe. "Why?" she asked. "If King Croesus over here wants to foot dinner, I'm not going to say no."

"Absolutely," said Ellis. "A fool and his money are soon parted anyway, so I might as well be on the receiving end."

Jack leaned over the table. "Bruce doesn't like it because it's dirty money."

"How so?"

He told them where he got the money, and I took a moment of satisfaction when they looked appalled. But then Ellis said, "I never get that lucky. I never find windfalls like that."

"You ought to be ashamed of yourself," Carrie said, "and for penance I think you *should* pay for our suppers. Right, Theresa?"

Theresa looked at me, then at the three of them, and, like an asteroid influenced by the mass of a larger planet, gravitated to them. "I guess so," she said.

I shook my head. "Not mine."

"Oh, good grief, Bruce," said Carrie, "don't be a goober."

"I'm not a goober, Carrie; I just wouldn't feel right about it."

Jack flicked his fingers at me and said, "What are you, trying for sainthood or something? Whoever heard of Saint Bruce?"

"Imagine him with a miter and crosier," said Carrie. Ellis snorted. Jack held up his hand in the Boy Scout salute and said, *"Domine Patri et Fili et Spiritu Sancti. . . ."*

The Book of PROVERBS

Be not thou envious against evil men,
neither desire to be with them.
—Proverbs 24:1

I'm not even *Catholic*.

When I was younger, I read a book about Saint Francis of Assisi in Sunday school and I thought it was great that he could talk to animals, but I never thought any more about saints than that. In our church we don't seem to go on about them much.

After Jack and company got started calling me Saint Bruce, everybody picked it up, friends and foes alike. My friends do it to show they like me, I guess, and the people who *don't* like me—well, they'd twist anything. Even Coach Donne got wind of it, and now I have to suffer through "Get the lead out, Saint Bruce" every time I go to PE.

I don't like it; it gives me the kind of feeling you

get when you're given somebody else's prize at a contest. But it would have been pointless to argue with Coach Donne, who responds to most challenges with "Drop and give me twenty."

Maybe sainthood is something you're just not supposed to complain about. Maybe that's why the church waits fifty years after someone has died to call them a saint—fewer arguments.

Still, "Saint Bruce" is better than "Number 24." That's Mr. Farmer's name for me. Mr. Farmer teaches typing, and before each hour of clicking racket he calls the roll by number. An example:

"Number 22," intoned Mr. Farmer.

"Here," said Paul Vincent.

"Number 23."

"Here," answered Chelsea Wallace.

"Number 24."

"I am not a number. I am a free man."

That was me. Have you ever seen *The Prisoner?* It's about this secret agent who retires, but they think he's going to defect, so they kidnap him and take him to this weird place called The Village. In The Village, he's only known as Number 6, and his will never, never breaks. At the beginning of the show, he always says, "I am not a number. I am a free man." I like that. Mr. Farmer looks at me over his bifocals and says, "If you are present, Mr. Wells, please signify by saying 'here.' "

I say "here," and he always pauses and says, "Conformity, Mr. Wells, is the oil in the cogs of society, and the nonconformist is the pebble in the shoe of the world." But he knows I refuse to be just like everybody else, and I think it livens up his day.

One day when our class was typing away (mostly using two fingers—the hunt-and-peck method), the intercom popped on. The principal, Mrs. Tatum (traditionally, Carthage North High students have called her "the Tater"), cleared her throat so everyone could hear.

"Attention, please," she said. And after a moment, "Attention, please." Another wait. "The pep rally will begin in ten minutes in the gym, so will all students and faculty begin to assemble there at this time. Teachers, please keep this orderly. . . ."

Not a hope.

It was like Hercules diverting the rivers to clean the Augean stable, except with teenagers instead of water. The halls filled, surged, and drained gymward in a matter of minutes. I was one of the last to leave typing class, and I heard Mr. Farmer grumble, "Such a waste of time. Such a waste of valuable time."

That made me think, as I dragged myself toward the gymnasium.

I despise pep rallies. Why is everybody in the entire school expected to chant like pagans to support the football team? Why do they—"they" being the spirit-minded Mrs. Tatum—assume we all care whether the football team wins or loses? Is there no middle ground? What of the people who can take it or leave it? What of the people who would rather peel their fingernails off than sit through a game?

At the pep rally, I found a seat on the groaning bleachers between Brad McColl and my friend Carrie. I know Brad only slightly. He's a thin, effeminate guy everybody says is gay—brutal rumor most likely—but Carrie is . . . Carrie.

As the rally reached gale force, Ellis climbed up and sat behind us with an aloof nod. The bleachers began shaking to the thump of the band's drums and the blasting of its trumpets. Was it music? Experts disagree.

Carrie leaned her head toward me and shouted something.

"What?" I said. Her tone was sarcastic, but her words were unclear.

"----------!"

"What? Speak up!"

"----------!!"

Then a great roar arose as the cheerleaders bounded onto the floor like circus performers, accompanied by the band.

What an extravaganza. Never have so few been so deafened by so many in so short a time for so little reason. Ruth Hightower, a cheerleader, flounced in front of the bleachers where I sat, bellowing with the others, "Give me a C!"

To which the brainwashed masses replied, "C!"

"Give me an A!"

"A!"

I sat immobile. Ruth singled us out of the crowd (perhaps because we were among the few not convulsing) and motioned for us to join in the cheer. I stared, mute as a swan, defying her with my entire being. At my side, scorn for the whole proceeding rolled off Carrie in waves.

The rally lasted through the usual chants and the obligatory principal's speech, to wit: "Now we're going to get out there and beat (fill in the blank) High School tonight, so let's give our athletes a big cheer!"

Huzzah.

By the time the pep rally ended it was time for class change, so Carrie, Ellis, and I walked together to Mrs. Atwell's room for our Latin class. We three always shared a corner of the room with Jack and Theresa. As soon as we arrived, Jack started in: "Did you get a whiff of Anna Roberts when she went by?"

Ellis raised a thin eyebrow. "No. What did she smell like?"

"She must have bathed in perfume. You could smell it clear down the hall."

Carrie slid into her desk. "I wouldn't talk, Jack. I've been on dates with guys who use so much cologne it stinks."

"I use a little cologne," Ellis said, "but only a very little."

Theresa said, "Mom lets me use some of her perfume too." She was about to say more, but her voice tapered out. Theresa's sentences always sounded like they were a sweater coming unraveled.

"Do you use any, Bruce?" Carrie asked.

"No. I figure if we were meant to smell like that we would have been made that way. I mean, you hear in the Bible about people being anointed with sweet oil and stuff, but still . . ."

"Exactly," said Jack. " 'Vanity of vanities; all is vanity.' "

"I think that has to do with life being in vain, Jack."

"Oh. Well, all the same, God didn't make us to smell like flower fart, so why use chemicals?"

Ellis said, "You're assuming you don't smell like old laundry."

"Hey—why drown out your natural pheromones? Why change it if you already have a scent that drives women wild?"

"Oh. Stop me. Hold me back," said Carrie in a monotone.

Jack has been fascinated by pheromones ever since he read about them in a *Penthouse* magazine. Where he got it I don't know, but Jack is the kind of guy who has the brass to just walk right up and buy one. It's strange how some people can be so casual about that sort of thing. I was once on an airplane and I could see two guys in the seats in front of me with a sex magazine, and both reading it at the same time. People's behavior puzzles me.

Mrs. Atwell rapped her desk and the class got under way. *Lingua patriae nostrae non Latina est, sed Anglica,* and I, for one, am grateful that we speak English over Latin. Latin is so much more regimented than English. English seems more alive. But then, how can you say Latin is a dead language when it's used all the time by scientists, lawyers, and doctors? There's a lot I don't understand.

The five of us in our corner were pretty good with Latin, and we made up a big chunk of the Latin Club; it was really more social than academic. There were a few other people in it, but Jack, Carrie, Theresa, Ellis, and I were—I don't want to say a clique, because we weren't really cliquish—exclusive. Latin was our last class of the day, so we usually stayed afterward awhile and talked. Mrs. Atwell didn't mind; she just did her paperwork and let us hang around, but she listened and sometimes added to the discussion.

"My head is still throbbing from that pep rally," Carrie said that day. "Why are we made to go to those things?"

"Come on, Carrie," said Ellis, "where's your school spirit?"

"Same place as yours."

"They have their good points," said Jack. "Cheerleaders, for instance. Hey, Bruce, did you get a look at Ruth Hightower? Legs up to there."

I never know how to respond to this. No, I didn't notice Ruth's legs. Ruth is a nonentity, a vacuum-head.

Talking to her is like talking to a cabbage. Her mind doesn't interest me, so why should her legs?

Carrie looked at Jack with distaste. "Oh, why focus on just one body, Jack? There were so many to choose from."

Jack grinned. "Some are better than others. Did you notice that Jan Swenson didn't jump very high? I've heard she doesn't wear anything underneath."

"It's interesting," Carrie said, addressing the rest of us, "the way you can always tell what's going through Jack's mind at any given moment."

"*Shall* we change the subject?" said Ellis, leaning back in his desk.

"Explain something to me," I said. "What possessed the founders of this school to make our school mascot the Trojans?"

"Yeah, they lost," said Theresa.

"It was a self-fulfilling prophecy," Ellis said sagely. "It turned out they were right, didn't it? We've lost four games out of the last five we've played against the Carthage South Roosters."

"And why," said Carrie, "do we always build a Trojan horse for homecoming? The Trojan horse was built by the *Greeks*. It's stupid."

"Not everybody knows the classics as well as you do, studying Latin," said Mrs. Atwell from across the room. "You have to make some allowance for ignorance."

"Why?"

"Because you have to live with other people. *E pluribus unum*. It's not smart to set yourselves apart, and you five do it so easily. I wish you'd be a little more patient with the other students in the Latin Club. You tend to leave them behind, especially you, Ellis."

"The world is for the strong," Ellis said.

"I'm not sure I believe that. Anyway, this classroom is for the absent, because I've got to get home. See you all tomorrow."

There was another pep rally in a couple of weeks, only it was moved to the last class period because teachers had been complaining that pep rallies left students too hyper to learn anything in class afterward. So there was no Latin that day.

I got to the gym so late this time I had to take a seat right on the front bench next to Chris Arkin, who, evidently, is allergic to soap. The rah-rah-sis-boom-bah began in earnest, and the assault on ears and nose together made me squint. I thought of leaving (a recurring fantasy), but large male athletic coaches stood guard by the exits. Their motto is "Many come in, but few return to the sunlit realms."

Ruth Hightower seemed determined to get me to chant. She jounced up right in front of me, shook her pom-pom like a dust mop in my face, and shouted, "Give me a C!"

"*Q!*" quoth I. Yes, I did notice her legs at this range. I noticed she had cut herself shaving.

Mrs. Tatum interrupted the chaos twice to ask that no more paper planes be thrown out onto the floor. On pain of death, one presumed. Then the rustle of pom-poms continued, followed by the construction of a human pyramid. Sort of.

Maybe I'm being too hard on them all. Maybe it's unfair of me to expect more of them than this bellowing, jostling, and climbing atop one another like young dogs. I'm willing to consider that I might be unfair. But consider the mob behavior: at last year's annual-signing day, the principal made an (ill-advised) attempt to change the way we get our annuals. She made an announcement that students were to form a line in front of room 213, where the annuals were to be handed out.

There are 1,627 students in our school.

There was a stampede.

I admit it, I ran with the rest of them, and got well situated in line, about twenty people from the front. But each of these twenty people had two friends who wanted to cut into line, and each of these friends had two friends, and soon I had been backed around the corner. Mild man of science Mr. Hughes had to bellow threats of mass execution before there was any kind of order.

Does that sound like sour grapes because I got pushed back, or worse, because I didn't have any friends who wanted in front of *me?* I guess it might sound that way, but at the time I remained philosophical. I had paid for an annual; I would receive an annual; there was plenty of time to get it signed.

I walked out of that pep rally thinking that Mr. Farmer had hit the nail a solid whack on the head. Nearly an hour of my life had gone by, and to what profit? Our days, hours, minutes—nay, *seconds*—are numbered, and this school not only expects me to use my short, precious time on this earth to spur our school team on to victory, but requires it!

(We lost, that night, to the Morrisville Yellow Devils, 42–7.)

The Latin Club met after school the next Monday, and the five of us sat back and listened to the old business, of which there was little, and the new business, of which there was less. We were not the officers, you understand; Carrie said politics were beneath her, Ellis had already done it once, and the others tended to follow his lead. Theresa was the exception. She got elected sergeant at arms (whatever that is). Poor Theresa. She wanted to be part of a group so badly that she ended up on the fringes of all of them.

"The last item of new business," said Chuck Callis, the club president, "is the float for the homecoming parade this year. Since we're the Latin Club I move that we do a Trojan horse. Anybody second?"

"Second!" seconded Terri Ortega. If seconds were six-guns, they could have used Terri at the OK Corral.

"Dear God." That was Carrie, muttering. Even Ellis, usually so cold, so cool, so aloof, shook his head.

"I think we should secede," said Carrie. We stayed after the meeting for a meeting of our own, just the five of us. Theresa had been torn between staying with us and going out with the rest to begin collecting chicken wire and newspapers, but she stayed because Ellis had given her a withering look.

"I'm not building any Trojan horse," Jack agreed. "That's for certain."

"Of course not," said Ellis. "We'd be a laughing-stock except that none of the idiots at this school knows the difference."

Theresa said, "I know it's not historical, but it is kind of traditional. . . ."

Ellis snorted. "So is unidentifiable lunch meat. So is square dancing in PE. So are pep rallies. That doesn't mean they make any sense."

"I've been thinking about that," I said.

"Hear the word of Saint Bruce," Jack cut in. I elbowed him.

"Why should we be *forced* to go to pep rallies?" I said. "Who here actually likes them?"

"I do," said Theresa. "Sort of. Not really," she finished, seeing our faces.

I said, "We ought to petition the principal to be excused."

"You mean let out of school?" Jack was interested.

"I don't see the Powers going for that," said Ellis.

"No, but maybe they'd let us stay in class and study, or something."

"Study!" said Jack. "Get real. Who's going to sign on to that?"

"Me, for one. Wouldn't you, to get out of going to those shouting matches?"

"But . . . studying . . ."

"This is inspired," said Carrie, ignoring Jack. "A protest. We demand to be allowed to use the time for homework. It could work."

"I don't know," said Ellis. Ellis Blanton likes to be the alpha and omega of all we do. He turned his cool gaze on me, then looked out the window, frowning.

The Book of JACK

For their hearts studieth destruction,
and their lips talk of mischief.
—Proverbs 24:2

*T*his is going to be the greatest thing since Roger Purlow led the classic food fight two years ago," said Jack as we walked into the gym. We weren't headed for a pep rally this time, but for another dehumanizing hour of physical education. Physical *education?* It's nothing but a golden opportunity for the jocks to lord it over the rest of us.

"Jack, you make it sound like we're about to have a huge snowball fight instead of a petition."

"I've always wanted to have one of those. You know, a good six-inch snow and five people on each side, with snow forts. Snow wars."

Jack opened the door to The Locker Room, and I steeled myself before going in.

Imagine a man faced with the prospect of entering a place where his very self would be exposed to scorn and scrutiny, where his dignity would be peeled away as though it were the skin on a banana; would he go willingly? You understand my feeling, then, toward The Locker Room.

Jack, maddeningly, doesn't mind it, and why should he? He's a decent athlete, though not great, and can bench 175 pounds. Is "bench" really a verb? Also, he's got a great build and the face of a Greek god. I, on the other hand, have failed profoundly in any sport you would care to name. I repel all balls—footballs, volleyballs, baseballs, basketballs, tennis balls, and Ping-Pong balls. Chris Arkin is hugely fat and picks his nose, and yet people choosing teams routinely argue over him if the loser is going to get me. That's not sour grapes, it's the truth. I tell myself it's all just a nuisance, not painful, not spirit crushing. I tell myself I'm not really even interested in sports and couldn't care less about "benching" 225 like Kurtis Dixon. That's what I tell myself.

As we walked in, Jack high-fived Kurtis Dixon. Why do people do that? Is it some kind of primitive, instinctive bonding ritual? When I escape from here and go to college, I think I'll become a behavioral scientist so I can find out what it all means.

I brought clean gym clothes from home today, but Jack fished his (reeking) shorts and T-shirt from his locker. The dressing out began.

"Hey, Kurtis," Jack said. "You're on the football team; what do you get out of pep rallies?"

Jack wastes no time.

"Well, I tell you," said Kurtis. Kurtis Dixon always begins his sentences with these same four words. "It's like everybody out there is looking at me and the guys and likes us, see, and they're building us up for the game. And when you see some babe yelling her head off for you, it's really great." He adjusted his jockstrap. "The cheerleaders aren't bad either. Like when I had Ruth Hightower back behind the bleachers after a game and she slipped off her bra—"

We interrupt this fascinating retelling of sexual adventures to bring you a word from our sponsor, the country music industry. Dad listens to country music all the time, and the other day I heard a song that went, in part, "A boy became a man that night . . ." If someone had walked into The Locker Room and said, "Hey, I hear Kurtis became a man last night," it would have started a round of butt slapping, rib elbowing, and coarse praise. On the other hand, if someone had said, "Bruce became a man last night," most of the guys would have had to untangle their eyebrows where they'd raised them up into their hairlines. Why are most guys congratulated for this?

I asked Jack once, and he said, "Saint Bruce, I don't know whether you think too much, or not enough. When you do something most other guys are dying to do, you're in. And for most other guys, getting in the sack is pretty high on the list."

"But why?"

He sighed. "If I have to explain it, you're not going to understand."

I don't, and that scares me.

We've been playing basketball, heaven help me, for the last two weeks. After an hour of skillfully maneuvering myself away from the action on the court, in spite of Coach Donne hollering, "Mix it up, Saint Bruce!" we all head (mercifully) back into The Locker Room to shower and change.

Jack had the fever once we left the gym. Even in The Locker Room, that bastion of athletic pep, he had managed to preserve his own conviction that we were onto something.

"We've got to plan this thing," he told me, scribbling in his notebook. "We've got to sit down with the others and work out just how to carry this thing across to the Powers."

"Would it be possible to eat our lunch first?" I said. "I'm starving."

"Well, that's a switch. You're always saying I'm the one with a hollow leg. All right, we'll find Carrie and Ellis and sit with them. We'll hash this out over the slops."

Jack and I share the first lunch shift, right after PE, with Carrie and Ellis. Theresa has third lunch, but she doesn't add much to the conversations anyway. We decided to fill her in after Latin.

An observation: pasta should never be served in school cafeterias. It ends up like white bread soaked in water. It's hard to tell where one noodle ends and another begins, and macaroni and cheese looks like some kind of whipped yellow pâté. Jack asked the cook for a double serving of that and a chuck-wagon patty.

I shuddered and took chicken, chips, and pudding—fairly safe—and followed him around the lunchroom until we spied Ellis and Carrie in the corner. Ellis had his chin propped in his hand, while Carrie tackled some physics homework, doubtless due next period.

Ellis nodded at us, unsmiling, and Carrie muttered a hello as we sat. Jack set his tray on the table, then leaned over and poked Carrie's plastic fork into the base of her Styrofoam cup. It didn't leak, but if she pulled it out her lemonade would drain everywhere. Jack always does that. I think he likes Carrie.

"Jack," she said, glancing at the cup and then back to her physics, "you are a moron."

"Thank you. Listen, we were just playing basketball with Kurtis Dixon in PE—"

"*You* were playing," I said.

"—and I got him to admit that he would probably play just as well even if there weren't any pep rallies."

I had missed this, keeping out of the way, but I remembered that Jack had stayed close to Kurtis the whole game.

"Are we on pep rallies again?" said Ellis, still propped on his hand.

"Unless you'd rather talk about your sex life."

"Not really." Ellis shifted his position, but he kept his hand on his chin. "But I don't think you'll ever get out of going to the rallies."

"We might as well try though," Jack said through a mouthful of macaroni. "Saint Bruce here hates them, and I just don't like being forced."

"Will you quit calling me that?"

"I think pep rallies are a plot," said Carrie, finishing her last problem and closing her book. "They're a blatant plot by the front office to pacify the student body and make them more susceptible to conservative propaganda."

"Don't you mean, make *us* more susceptible?" said Ellis.

"*We're* not falling for it. *We're* the ones planning the revolution."

Jack said, "Ellis, what's the matter with you? You haven't moved your hand off your chin since we got here."

"Does it bother you?"

"He's got a zit," Carrie explained. Ellis shot her a freezing look.

"Quiet," he said.

"Yeah?" said Jack. "Let's see it."

"I don't think so."

"Oh, come on, El. It can't be that bad. We all get them, except for Saint Bruce of the Holy Skin. It must be all that clean living—no whiskey and no women."

"Jack, can it," I said. "I do, too, get them. Shut up and eat your macaroni." Ellis's mood was blackening before my eyes, and he saw me watching.

"Nobody's that pure," he said. He would have said more, but Carrie knocked on the table.

"Let's get back to the pep rally business. It seems to me it's going to be pretty simple to explain that we want the right to use our time to study instead of shouting brainlessly at a pep rally. The tough part is going to be getting a teacher to sponsor us. They're never going to let us loose on our own."

"That's a point," said Jack, sawing on his chuck-wagon steak. The aroma made me queasy. "Who can we get?"

"All teachers are required to go to the pep rallies to help with riot control," said Ellis.

"Mr. Farmer hates them," I said, spooning my pudding. "I heard him say they're a waste of valuable time."

Carrie spread her hands. "There! A kindred spirit."

"Yeah," Jack said, thinking. "Old MacDonald might do it. Who's going to ask him?"

"We need to send a delegation, not just one person," said Carrie.

"I might as well go, since I've got him for class," I said.

Jack looked around the table, then shrugged. "I guess I'll go too. I had him last semester. He nearly flunked me, but we got along all right."

"Fine." Carrie wiped her mouth. "But if we're going to do this right, we need a name for all of us. We can't be just a bunch of students. We've got to have a label."

"It was Bruce's idea," said Jack. "We're the Disciples of Saint Bruce."

"Oh, come on," I protested, but Carrie was too full of her own designs to listen.

"I like that," she said. "Ellis?"

Ellis's eyes flicked over us, narrowing as they settled on me. "Whatever," he said.

A little Yahootie in my head kept whispering, "You are *not* a saint." But they kept on, and it's hard to argue with someone who says you can do no wrong.

Jack and I planned to be at school early the next day. We met by the Guidance Office door, just down the hall from Mr. Farmer's class, and watched him go in.

"Do you think this'll work?" Jack asked.

"How should I know?"

"This could be our Waterloo."

"But we might be Wellington."

He thought about that, then smiled. "Old MacDonald could say no, then go and bust us to the Tater."

"It's not as though we're planning a school coup," I said.

"You know what I like about you? You're always

foolishly trying to get the best out of the worst. Me, I like to see the potential for disaster. It lets you feel like you're living on the edge. Women like a man who lives on the edge."

"Can we just go?"

We went.

Mr. Farmer sat hunched at his desk, leafing through student papers with little sad shakes of his head. Jack cleared his throat.

"Mr. Farmer, could we talk to you for a minute?"

He looked up, over his bifocals. "Ah. Number 11. You were with me last semester, weren't you?"

"Uh, yeah. Yes, sir."

"Yes. I remember you, Mr.—"

"LaRue."

"Yes. And Number 24—"

"I am not a number. I am a free man."

Mr. Farmer showed his teeth in a tiny, level grin, as though he were pulverizing a cranberry seed between his incisors. "Yes, Mr. Wells. And Mr. LaRue. What can I do for you?"

We had earlier agreed, against my better judgment, to let Jack do the talking, so he started right in. "Mr. Farmer, we were wondering what you think about pep rallies."

Mr. Farmer cocked an eyebrow. "That's an odd question."

We waited.

"They are a mandatory activity," he continued.

"All students and faculty are required to assemble in the gymnasium to cheer on our school's team."

"Yes, sir, but what do *you* think of them? I mean, what do you *think?*"

He swiveled his chair around so that he faced us fully. "I have never really followed school sports," he said, "not even when my own son was in high school. I cannot say I share any great enthusiasm for athletics." He spoke slowly, as though he was guarding every word, as though he wasn't sure they ought to be coming out of his mouth.

Jack said, "Would you say that pep rallies were a waste of time, for some people?"

Mr. Farmer glanced keenly from him to me. "I . . . could think of better ways to spend an hour. More productive ways."

Jack grinned. I could see the tension slip off his shoulders. "So can we. There are five of us who want to petition the principal to let us off pep rallies to use the time to study, and we need a teacher to sponsor us. Will you do it?"

Jack is like a bomb with a delayed fuse. He can only hold back for so long before his enthusiasm carries him away, far away. Mr. Farmer pressed back into his chair. He picked up a pencil and put it down again, then shuffled some papers.

"I'm flattered . . . flattered," he said, "but no, no, I think. No."

Jack sagged. "Why, sir?"

"Because . . ." Here Mr. Farmer steadied himself, then spoke very evenly. "Let me tell you something about this school, and about life, really. It's something I've tried to hammer into Mr. Wells, here, to no avail. You will get along with everyone much better if you don't upset the egg carton. Don't monkey with tradition. You'll only get the worst of it, and if not you, then somebody else. No. I'm sorry, gentlemen, but I'm afraid I must refuse. I'm very flattered, but no. And now, I suggest you get to your homerooms. The bell is about to ring."

We left, making no great speed to beat the bell. Jack's eyes were wide. After we had gone a ways down the hall, he looked at me and said, "Bruce, he has a son! Can you imagine Old MacDonald and his wife doing the Wild Thing?"

"Jack! He said no!"

"Man, who would have thought?"

"Get your mind out of the gutter for a minute. We've been set back; we've got no sponsor. Carrie will chew nails."

"Oh, lighten up. We'll just ask somebody else."

"Hm. Maybe. I was just so sure Mr. Farmer would agree."

"It's not the end of the world. 'All these things must come to pass, but the end is not yet.' You ought to know that, O sainted friend of mine."

"Quit it. What are you, the Pope? Going around sainting people."

Jack held up his Boy Scout salute and made a cross in the air. *"Domine Patri et Fili et Spiritu Sancti . . ."*

I looked at my watch. "Come on, I don't want to be tardy for the first day of my school career."

"You've *never* been tardy?"

"Well, once . . ."

"That's disgusting. Live a little, you prig."

"I love you too. Listen, I'll see you in PE. We'll talk about who else to ask then."

"How about the obvious person?"

"Who's that?"

"Mrs. Atwell. You've seen her at pep rallies with her fingers in her ears. And besides, she likes us, and you particularly. She's bound to sponsor us."

"I wouldn't say she likes me *particularly*. Anyway, we'll talk about it in gym."

"Yeah. Man, do you suppose they sleep in the same bed?"

"What?"

"Old MacDonald and the Mrs."

"Jack!"

Jack shrugged and ducked into his homeroom. I sprinted the last few yards to my homeroom and slipped in the door to the jangle of the bell.

The Book of AGRICOLA

Through wisdom is an house builded;
and by understanding it is established.
—Proverbs 24:3

My *sister, Lee Ann,* is in junior high, and she is a rock-and-roll fiend. She has wallpapered her room with posters of people more bizarre than any ever seen in the pages of *National Geographic.* She keeps her stereo cranked up so loud it makes the walls shake. Not long ago I took her to a concert (*I* certainly didn't want to go, but it was her birthday) and was deafened.

Why do people do that? What is so enjoyable about sitting among thousands of people screaming to be heard over the ground-shaking music they're supposed to be listening to? Mom told me, "Oh, we did the same thing when we were your age. It's a kind of rebellion."

Rebellion? How can anybody claim to be noncon-formist standing in a mob of thousands doing exactly the same thing? And look at the lyrics, a lot of which center around a theme of "oh-baby-can't-live-without-you." Well, yes, you can. It's done all the time. Romeo and Juliet were not a typical case. It seems to me that the real rebellion is in not buying into popular music at all, even when it's forced on you.

Take jukeboxes—please. Why do people in restaurants assume that their choice of dining music is the same as everybody else's? How do they know their music isn't going to put somebody off his lunch? Do they even care?

I only ask these questions because the day after our interview with Mr. Farmer I walked into PE and found the girls had begun doing aerobics to rock music, and I knew I was condemned to listen to it not just for the next hour, but for the next two weeks. A bad sign of things to come.

I found Jack, and we decided to put the prospect of Mrs. Atwell sponsoring us to a meeting of the Disciples before approaching her. This would give us time to soften her up.

The chance came right after Latin. Ellis had to go straight home after school, Carrie had a five-paragraph theme to work on, and Theresa, the joiner, had to go to a Key Club meeting, so there was no way to gather the five of us to talk about the plan.

"It's stupid for just you and me to meet," Jack said. "We already know everything we would talk about. Let's scratch it until tomorrow."

I agreed, and after class Jack ran out to his car in the seniors' parking lot, but Mrs. Atwell flagged me down going out the door.

"Bruce, I want to talk to you for a minute, please," she said. Mrs. Atwell doesn't call me Saint Bruce. We talk, sometimes, after school. Sometimes she tells me about her family, and I tell her about mine, but most of the time she asks what other students say and think.

"You're my finger on the pulse of the teenage world," she told me. Today was a pulse check.

"Bruce," she said, "I wonder if I could ask you a question about Ellis."

"Ellis? I guess so."

"Have you ever heard him say what it's like at home?"

"At his house? No. Ellis doesn't say much about that. Well . . ." She nodded encouragement. "It's just gossip, you know, but I've heard a couple of people say his dad has a temper. I don't know that it's true."

Mrs. Atwell tapped her temple absently with the point of her pencil, looked at it, flipped it around to the eraser, and tapped again. "That would explain," she said.

I didn't ask what, but I didn't need to.

"I know I can trust you not to say anything," she said, "because I'm not really supposed to discuss something like this with students, but Ellis's quizzes and homework haven't been his best work lately. I thought there might be some problem at home."

"Oh."

"I know you won't say anything. You might try to cheer him up next time you see him though. He might need it."

Cheering up Ellis was a tall order, but I left happy that she held me in her confidence. It wasn't so much a pleasure at being trusted, just a pride that she'd picked *me* for it.

I had got way down the hall before I realized I hadn't done any softening up. I started back, but Mr. Farmer stuck his head out of his room.

"Number 24, would you join me for a moment?"

"I am not a number. I am a free man."

"All the same, Mr. Wells . . ."

He sat at his desk and gestured for me to take a seat in the front row. He had put all the covers on the typewriters. As he talked he began to clean his glasses with some eyeglass cleaner and a tissue.

"I hope I did not seem uncivil when I spoke to you and Number 11 earlier."

"Jack."

"Hm?"

"His name is Jack."

"Oh, yes. Mr. LaRue. But that's not what I meant, calling you by numbers. I meant my behavior after you had made your request."

"I didn't think you were uncivil, sir."

"Nevertheless, I feel I should explain. You are not the first to have asked, you see."

He must have seen my surprise even without his glasses, for he sighed and slipped them back on.

"Mr. Wells, I have been at this school for a long time. Only Mrs. Embry in art has been here longer, and I dare say even she hasn't noticed, as I have, how everything is the same, no matter how many times the faces change. I doubt she would remember the time, and it wasn't so many years ago, that the last bunch of students asked to be excused from pep rallies."

"Really? How long ago?"

"Eight, nine years. Something like that. No, nine, because Mr. Cole has had Mr. Travers's wood shop class for that long. It was on account of what happened that Mr. Travers had to go." Mr. Farmer leaned forward across his desk. "Seven students had asked Mr. Travers to agree to keep them in his room during pep rallies so they could study. He agreed. But one afternoon he left them on their honor because he needed to attend a conference, and the students took their opportunity and left school early. No one would have known except that one of the students' parents caught them in town and reported it to the school. It was a very serious breach at the time."

Why was he telling me this? I wanted to say, "That was then and this is now." Instead, I said, "None of us are like that."

Mr. Farmer slapped his desk with his palm. "Yes, you are," he said. *"Yes, you are.* I see this time and again—young people have the notion that they are one of a kind, that they are a completely new and different variety, that they are the first to come up with this or that new idea. But each of you is only the latest of a long line of people just like you. There is nothing new under the sun. Do you imagine, Mr. Wells, that you are the first person ever to have quoted that line from *The Prisoner* during roll call? Number 17 did the exact same thing six years ago; I don't remember his name, but he quoted it verbatim as you do."

I got a sinking feeling. He must have seen that too.

"Not as clever as you thought, are you?"

"Well," I returned, "every person is unique in his own way."

"Where did you learn that? *Mister Rogers' Neighborhood?* You, like all the rest of us, are only unique in the particular combination of commonplacenesses that make you up. Every single aspect of you is duplicated in some other person; only the way those aspects are gathered together separates you from other individuals. It's like snowflakes."

"But no two snowflakes are alike."

"On the contrary. Individual snowflakes only differ in the minutiae. All snowflakes are basically identical, reacting within the limits nature has set on frozen water. Appearance aside, they are ice, each and every one, and will never behave in any way except the way ice must behave. Human beings are no different. We are not infinitely variable. And that, young man," he said, shaking a finger at me, "is why history repeats itself. And that is why I felt I had to refuse your request. I do not think you and your friends are any more apt to take advantage than any of your peers, but it has been known. And it was a shame about Mr. Travers."

Mr. Farmer began gathering papers off his desk and placing them tidily in his briefcase. He seemed finished, so I rose.

"One more thing, Mr. Wells," he said. He held one of my papers from typing. "Your speed has improved, but not your accuracy. An orangutan could do as well. Practice. Practice!"

"The old fart."

That was Jack's comment when I told him what Mr. Farmer said. We five had convened a meeting after Latin the next day. Mrs. Atwell had had to go to a faculty meeting, but we expected her back anytime. We would pop the question today.

"Why is he teaching if he hates people our age?" said Ellis. He had been to the convenience store on the corner and had come back with a pop, and was now sipping it through a straw.

"I don't think he hates us," I said. "He just thinks we're not serious."

Carrie was writing out our speech to Mrs. Tatum in her notebook. "If history really repeats itself like he says," she said, "then we're bound to get the okay for this, since the last people who asked got it. It's logical."

"Yeah," said Jack, "and once we've got it, all we have to do to break the loop is not cut school."

Theresa looked startled. "We wouldn't do that anyway, would we?"

Carrie sighed. "We can't do *anything* that would cause us to lose the privilege."

"We can't get *caught*," Ellis said.

I opened my mouth to ask Ellis what he meant, but Mrs. Atwell returned, and you could feel the air around us close in; conspiratorial air. Looks passed between us. No one spoke. Jack nudged me in the arm.

"She likes you best," he said.

Carrie's eyes said *Go*.

Theresa had her hands clasped close to her, excited, but Ellis only stared, unreadable. At last he muttered, "Your move."

I stood up.

I walked across the room to her desk and stood there until she looked up.

"Yes, Bruce?"

I could feel four presences concentrated on me from across the room. "Mrs. Atwell, we have something we want to ask you. None of the five of us like pep rallies; in fact, we hate being forced to go to something we don't care anything about. We'd rather spend the time here studying, and we wondered if you would agree to sponsor us."

You have something weighty to say, something momentous, something that will shake the world, and then you say it and it comes out like the inside of an egg. Plop.

Mrs. Atwell shifted her eyes from me to them and back. "I've never heard of anybody who wanted out of pep rallies," she said. "Most people want *in*, to get out of class."

"We don't care anything about football."

"Or basketball?"

"Or basketball. We'd rather stay here."

"*Veritas?*" she said.

"Truly."

She joined her hands and put both thumbs to her lips as she always did when thinking. "I'm not sure Mrs. Tatum would agree," she said after a moment. "She's big on school spirit, and teachers are supposed to be there to keep order."

We waited.

"Well," she continued, "it can't hurt to ask. I don't like them either."

Jack whooped; even Ellis's mouth turned up. Carrie came forward and showed our speech to Mrs. Atwell, who looked it over.

"This is all right, Carrie, but you might lower the language."

"What do you mean?"

"I wouldn't begin it 'Oyez, oyez.' Just be businesslike and to the point."

"Oh, okay." Carrie scribbled herself a note in the margin.

"When can we ask Mrs. Tatum?" said Jack.

"If you want this to take effect before the next rally, we'd better do it tomorrow."

So, the next day, after the last bell, we gathered at Mrs. Atwell's door and trooped as one body to the front office. Mrs. Atwell told the secretary we wanted to see Mrs. Tatum, and after a minute we were shown into her office.

I had never, in four years of high school, been in the principal's office. I'm neither one of those who gets to see it for doing the wrong thing, nor one of those who gets to see it for doing the right thing. The first thing I saw now was a huge pennant reading "Go Carthage North Trojans" hung point down on the wall. This boded ill.

Have you ever been given an award you had to walk onstage to receive? The moment builds and builds, and then afterward, you can hardly remember being up there. This was like that. Carrie read our petition; she had got rid of the beginning and mercifully any mention of the name they'd given our group. Mrs. Tatum listened, watching us with the eyes of a crocodile.

After Carrie finished, Mrs. Tatum said, "Everyone is required to attend the pep rallies. It helps support your fellow students whose efforts reflect on the school."

Carrie had anticipated this, and fielded it easily.

"We understand that, Mrs. Tatum, but when we go to college and then get jobs, our efforts will also reflect on the school, and we want to make Carthage North look good. Academics are our way of showing spirit, since we don't actually play or watch sports."

Jack nudged me behind Ellis's back, and pinched his nose as though he smelled something. I scowled at him and tried to look serious.

"And how do you feel about this, Mrs. Atwell?" Mrs. Tatum asked.

"I think we should consider the feelings of those who would prefer academia to athletics," said Mrs. Atwell. "This is an educational institution first and foremost, after all."

Mrs. Tatum was quiet for a minute.

"I will give your petition some thought," she said finally, "and let you know."

There was nothing more to say. Mrs. Atwell deftly herded us back into the front office, and we went our ways from there. When we came out, Mr. Farmer was making copies at the photocopier. His back was to us, but I could see him looking at our reflection in the window glass.

The next day I came in to Latin class just before the bell, and slid into my desk as Mrs. Atwell commenced writing a story in Latin on the board for us to translate. I sat back, surprised, to see that it was titled *"Magister Agricola"*—"Master Farmer." I thought maybe . . .

But later she began returning old papers and I found a note clipped to mine in her round script: PETITION APPROVED—P. A. I thought P. A. must mean Pamela Atwell, but later she explained she had meant *per auctoritatem*—by authority (of Mrs. Tatum).

Whatever.

We had done it.

In two weeks, Mrs. Tatum came on the intercom and said, "Will all students and teachers please begin to assemble in the auditorium for the pep rally. Teachers, please supervise. No running in the halls." Mrs. Atwell's class emptied like water down a drain, leaving the five of us, and Mrs. Atwell, sitting there.

Carrie said, breaking the sudden quiet, "It's hard to know what to do."

Mrs. Atwell snapped out of it. "Get out whatever work you brought with you to do," she said, "and get started."

The Book of ELLIS

And by knowledge shall the chambers
be filled with all precious and
pleasant riches.
—Proverbs 24:4

Why is it that my mother, whom I have
lived with for seventeen years, cannot remember that
I will not eat asparagus? It's pale green and slimy, and
the taste—oof! But time and again she'll say, "Who
wants some asparagus? Bruce?"

I long ago gave up trying to train her (she's untrain-
able), but I've never stopped wondering why I can't
stand asparagus. It's not one of those things you *learn*
to hate; I've had *that* happen twice. The first time was
when I was little. I ate two huge walnut sundaes at
one sitting and got rolling sick, and I haven't been
able to smell walnuts since without being queasy. The
second time was on our trip to Mexico when I got
whatever stomach bug you get down there right after

I'd eaten a huge slab of fish. I don't eat fish now, at least not if it *smells* like fish.

My loathing for asparagus is different. I've despised it from the very first time I ate it. When I remind Mom, patiently, that I don't eat asparagus, she says, "Oh. Well, try it again. Maybe you'll change your mind." But I won't. I've never liked it, and I never will.

It's like that with some people, I think. There are people in the world *who just don't like you*, not because of anything you've done or said, and not because of your skin color or anything like that—they *just don't like you*. And never will. Like asparagus.

I don't think Ellis ever really liked me much. We went to the same middle school, but we never spoke. Even as freshmen here at Carthage North we never had reason to speak to each other. Only when we ended up in Latin was there any common ground between us, but that ground was a narrow, barren strip of land.

Ellis called me Saint Bruce like the others, but he made the "saint" sound mocking. He was no saint, that's for sure. He wore ridiculous black boots and an earring (I have nothing against earrings on guys, you understand, I just can't see wearing one myself) and quite unabashedly smoked in the guys' rest room. Sometimes I caught myself not approving of Ellis.

Ellis was one of those intelligences without anything to do, one of those bright guys who ought to have done better than spray painting lewd messages on the school entrance sign. Jack encouraged him, too, but Jack is an uncontrollable force of nature. Even so, I once saw Jack and Ellis mooning other cars from Ellis's brother's convertible. That had to be Ellis's idea; Jack is pretty wild and crazy, but he would have needed a push to go that far.

Ellis liked being behind the wheel, so to say. Last year he (somehow) got elected president of the Latin Club and ruled with an iron fist. We had a car wash and a bake sale—all his ideas—and took in enough money for a club trip to the Parthenon in Nashville, Tennessee. Ellis had wanted us to go to Italy, but Mrs. Atwell said that was out of the question. We did a lot, and had some fun, but I think most of us felt like Egyptian slaves building the Great Pyramid for the pharaoh.

Though he tried to get elected again this year, Ellis lost.

I guess that's part of the reason he didn't like me at the head of our pep rally campaign—he must have felt like he was losing his touch. Anyway, I wasn't even really the head. Carrie was the mastermind.

We spent two blissful pep rally Fridays in Mrs. Atwell's room, our tranquillity broken only by the occasional muted thump of the band's bass drums. Sometimes Theresa would look toward the gym, as though she could see through the walls. But then she would glance at the rest of us, and sigh, and get back to her work.

Sometimes we talked. We shared an air among us of superiority to the huddled masses down in the arena being fed to the lions. But Mrs. Atwell kept us working. After a couple more weeks, she spoke to all of us at the start of our session.

"In three weeks I've got to be out of town on Friday for my niece's wedding, and another pep rally is scheduled for that week. I'll leave a note for my substitute to let you five stay here during the rally. I trust you to look after yourselves for forty-five minutes."

I felt the same swelling of pride I always felt when Mrs. Atwell said she trusted me. I thought we all did. We talked about it later and agreed we were looking forward to our day on our own.

Then Carrie got the flu.

On Wednesday she went to the school clinic and they sent her home with a raging fever. On Friday her empty desk in the third row kept announcing its emptiness. Four of us seemed like too few, like those still there were only pretending.

Whatever bug she had must have been the Godzilla of viruses. She didn't come back until the next Thursday, pale and still coughing.

"Are you sure you're well enough to be back?" I asked her at lunch.

"I was getting behind," she told me.

Jack said, "So you're trying for sainthood too? Man, you're crazy to be here. I would have milked it for all it was worth. I wouldn't have been back for a month."

"That is the difference between me and you," Carrie said. "I didn't want to have to catch up, and anyway, I was bored out of my mind."

"I wouldn't be bored," Jack said, unwrapping a brownie. "I've got a stack of magazines under my bed to read."

"Skin magazines," Ellis said.

Jack placed his palm against his chest. "Ellis, my boy," he said through a mouthful of brownie, "you cut me to the quick."

"He only gets them for the articles," Ellis went on.

"Sh! Not around Saint Bruce. He has tender ears."

I kicked him under the table.

Carrie made a face, disgusted. "Women are not objects to be ogled," she said. "Why don't you come out of the Dark Ages and join the rest of us?"

"I could, but it wouldn't be as much fun."

Carrie was about to say something else, but she began coughing.

"Hey!" I said. "Would you mind covering your mouth?"

"Sorry."

It was as easy as that. By Monday my head felt even worse than when I took my sister to that concert. It throbbed, and I went through chills and sweats by turns. The school nurse sent me home, and there I stayed for a solid week. Mom, bless her, took good care of me. I had broth and warm lemonade for my throat, and pillows and every other kind of decadent comfort one usually gets from one's mom when ill, but late on the sixth day she tried to get me to swallow some soup—cream of asparagus—and put me on my guard until the worst had passed.

The next week I had licked my cough and was in pretty good shape. I went back to school on Monday and Jack, the fool, led three cheers for my return in Latin. After school he rounded up the five of us.

"Let's all drive into town and get a soda to celebrate the triumphant return of Saint Bruce," he suggested. "Bruce is driving."

"Is he buying?" asked Ellis.

"Are you buying?" asked Jack.

I sighed. "I suppose so."

It was raining, so we all ran out to my car and piled in. I pulled out of the senior lot with Jack, from the backseat, saying, "Gun it! Gun it, man! Let's hear you squeal tires," knowing perfectly well that I was as likely to burn rubber as I was to walk buck naked through the cafeteria during first lunch. The screech of tires would have set Theresa off into mad giggles anyway. I drove us toward the fast-food drag, and nobody said much. Then Ellis tapped me on the shoulder.

"You should have been with us Friday afternoon," he said.

I don't know what made me tense at that, maybe some small, different quirk in his voice, or maybe just the fact that he had actually touched me; but I gripped the wheel.

Jack snickered. "You want to know what Ellis did?" he asked.

"No," I said. "No, I don't."

"Oh, come on," said Ellis. "Tell him, Jack. You tell it best."

"Is it something bad?" I said, looking at Carrie in the seat beside me.

"Well . . . ," she said, rocking her hand up and down.

"We had a little party," said Ellis, leaning forward so that his chin rested on the back of my seat.

"I don't think I want to hear this," I said. My windshield wiper kept going back and forth in front of me, up and down like Mr. Farmer's pointing finger.

"Yes, you do," said Jack. "Mrs. Atwell was gone Friday. We had Miss Bracherd for a substitute, and you know how she is. She left us and went down to the pep rally, and Ellis said, 'The departure of Miss Bracherd is like the passing of the dodo bird—we won't be seeing any more of her.' And then, see, he pulls out this bottle he smuggled in."

"I don't want to hear this. I do *not* want to hear this," I said, but Jack wouldn't, or couldn't, shut up, and I couldn't do anything because I was in the middle of the road driving. I might as well have been in a straitjacket. But I don't know, maybe that's just an excuse. I didn't want to hear, but at the same time, I did. I wanted to know their secret, to be in, to be a part, and they were willing to tell me.

"It was Jack Daniel's—*whiskey*," said Theresa in a conspiratorial whisper.

Jack slapped the seat, chuckling. "Ellis was in the front of the room doing his Brando impersonation. You know, 'Someday, and this day may never come, I will ask you to do a favor for me.' We laughed our damn heads off."

"You should have seen Theresa," said Ellis. "Drunk off her ass."

"Theresa?" said Jack. "What about Carrie?"

I shot a surprised look at Carrie, and she blushed.

"Don't look so shocked, Bruce," she said. "It was kind of a celebration. Ellis said we'd never really celebrated the victory of our petition, and he just brought something so we could have a little toast."

"We certainly got toasted," said Jack, grinning in my rearview mirror.

"You should have been there," said Ellis to my ear.

I pulled into a fast-food place and we got our drinks at the drive through, then I pulled back onto the road. The talk shifted, as quickly and as thoroughly as though a signal had passed between them—to who had seen what movie, and whether we ought to go out Saturday. They had changed the subject.

I kept waiting for Jack or Ellis to say something more, but they said no more. There wasn't any more to say.

I wanted to know, but in spite of that wanting, I told them not to tell me. Please be witness to that.

The Book of REVELATION

A wise man is strong; yea, a man of knowledge increaseth strength.
—Proverbs 24:5

*T*hree days after they told me about their party, Mrs. Atwell asked me to stay a few minutes when Latin class was finished. Ellis looked at me on his way out, but none of the other four had been asked to stay. Mrs. Atwell closed the door behind them.

"I'm glad you're feeling better, Bruce," she said. "I missed you in class. No ill effects, I hope?"

"No. I'm fine now. How was the wedding?"

"Oh, it was lovely. They went way overboard, of course, but you only get it once a lifetime."

"My uncle's with his third wife."

She considered this. "Well, maybe you get it more than once, but I don't think it's ever the same as the first time. It's a kind of threshold you cross, a time when you leave some things behind and become something different forever."

She opened her desk drawer and took something out, setting it on the desktop. I couldn't see what it was from where I sat.

"Bruce, when did you get sick?"

"Last Friday."

"And they sent you home?"

"Yes."

"For the whole week? You weren't here the day I was out?"

"No, I wasn't."

She picked the thing up and set it down again.

"Bruce, did Jack or Carrie say anything to you about last Friday?"

She was asking. I knew what she was asking, and I knew she knew I knew, but I didn't answer. I couldn't make a sound. I couldn't even move.

"Bruce, I have reason to think something happened last Friday that should never have happened. I don't want to believe it, but I need to know."

I was in a car with no brakes.

"You need to know what, ma'am?"

In a level voice, she said, "I need to know if they were drinking." She held out the thing she'd taken from her desk, waiting for me to come up and look at it. It was a piece of cellophane wrapping, from a bottle. It was black, with white letters that read "Old No. 7 brand Tennessee Whiskey."

"That was on the floor," she said. "Miss Bracherd found it when she came in to get her things after school."

I still couldn't say anything. To say anything except what she was waiting to hear would have been willing falsehood.

"Did you ask them about it?" I finally managed.

"They each denied having done anything. Yet there is still this," she said, fingering the wrapper. "Bruce, do you know what it could mean, if this was known?" she said. "I haven't been a teacher here that long. If they let the word get out that they'd been drinking in my class, in no time word would get back to some parent, and then I'd have to cover myself. Just in case I need a defense, I should know."

I told her. God help me.

Why do we want so much to be accepted? Why do we so yearn for others to appreciate us? I stood there, glad to be in her trust, and trusting her. She only wanted the information. She trusted me to tell her. Trust given is supposed to be returned.

I asked them not to tell me. I *begged* them. *Why* wouldn't they shut up? *Why* did they feel like they had to tell me what they'd done? *They* were the ones who called me Saint Bruce. They knew how I was.

But so did I. I could have stopped them—I could have kept shouting, or laid on the car horn or threatened to turn the car around. I'm not stupid. I could have thought of something.

How could they tell me something like that and not know what I would have to do with it? Knowing that, why did I let them?

When I came to school the next day, I didn't see Jack on the way to homeroom, which was strange; we always met on the way. I didn't see Jack or Carrie or Ellis at lunch. But on my way to PE, alone, I had to pass the corner near Mr. Farmer's room where the light is out in the hall and somebody shoved my shoulder against the lockers.

"You bastard."

Ellis blocked the light in front of me, a little taller in his black boots.

"Ellis?"

"You're so pure, aren't you? You're so lily-white. 'Saint Bruce'—what a crock. It must be hell to be you, all cramped up inside. No wonder you envy Jack; did you think nobody noticed how you envy him? Jack's the real man. He says what he thinks, even if it's not the 'right' thing. But you're so worried about being perfect that you've become a false man. You're no different from the rest of us inside, no matter what you do or say on the outside. So what if Jack talks with his gonads half the time? At least he's real. You get as horny as the rest of us; you just keep it covered up. Two-faced bastard."

"Ellis, what—"

He shoved me back against the lockers. The locker latch behind me dug into my ribs.

"Who did we hurt, Bruce? Who did we hurt? We just had a little fun. If you had been there, you would have done it too. You're no different than us."

I straightened up, and forced his hand back.

"You're wrong. You're right about a lot. But you're wrong this time. Nothing could have made me drink that."

The breath hissed out of his nostrils. "You either fall into step in life or you get the hell out of the way. Anything else you do hurts other people."

He stared at me in that shadowed corner, as coldly as I have ever been stared at or ever fear to be. Then he turned and walked away. My knees shook, but I made them hold me up as I walked past Mr. Farmer's door. Mr. Farmer was standing there, just inside, just standing.

In Latin none of them spoke to me. Theresa's eyes had swollen—she'd been crying. Carrie had a face of granite, and Jack only looked out the window. To Ellis, I had ceased to exist. Mrs. Atwell's face was unreadable. After class they all swept by me except Jack, who tapped me on the shoulder.

"I want to talk to you," he said. It was a demand.

We walked down the hall toward the gym, my friend and I, and he finally turned to the quiet hall where the janitors keep their brooms.

"We were suspended today," he said.

"What!"

"Until after Christmas. Mrs. Atwell reported us to the Tater. You told her, didn't you?" I opened my mouth, but to save my life I could not have said anything. "You don't have to answer," he said. "I don't know why, and I don't understand. I just thought better of you than that. I thought you were . . . you know . . ." His tone sounded almost pleading. "Man! I can't believe you told her! You're the saint!"

"You called me that, not me. What did you want me to be?"

He backed up, shouting, "I don't know! You're not like the rest of us. It's like you're not from Earth, you're so far from the reality of the rest of us. Poor Theresa had never had a drop in her life! She only drank because Ellis shamed her into it."

"What was your excuse? What was Carrie's?"

"I don't *need* an excuse. I just wanted to, that's all. It was just something to do. It was like living on the edge, okay? I can't say for Carrie, except that it's hard to be the odd man out." He crossed his arms. "You know what gets me about you?" he said. "You're just so neat. You *try* harder than anybody I've ever seen, and it's neat to see somebody actually *doing* what we all know we're supposed to do but don't. It makes people like us feel like we can be better. And now you do something like this. . . ." He waved his hand frustratedly.

"I asked you not to tell me."

He thought, and nodded. "Yeah. And we told you anyway. Can't you see we wanted you with us, Bruce? You were apart, and we wanted you to be a part of us. We were the Disciples of Saint Bruce. What were we without you? Ellis and Carrie would never have tolerated each other, neither one would have had anything to do with me, and Theresa would have been with her Key Club friends all along."

I blinked in surprise. I had never thought of myself as the hub of our group, just as another spoke.

Jack shifted his backpack on his shoulder and turned his side to me, to go. "This is my last day until after New Year's," he said. "Maybe I'll see you then. Tell Ruth I said hi."

He went, and an empty aching settled into me, and stayed.

When I next sat on the bleachers, I thought, There's got to be a reason why so many saints were martyred. I think that deep down, people really don't like themselves very much, and manage to live only by not looking at the parts they don't like. But if somebody comes along who makes them see those parts, they can't stand it, and have to either get rid of that person, or cause that person to be just like them. It's the only way they can live.

The bleachers shook as everybody jumped to their

feet. Ruth Hightower, in front of me, yelled, "Give me a C!"

"Jack says hi," I whispered.

The next day in Mr. Farmer's typing class, he handed back a paper to me covered with red marks, and with a note scrawled at the top: PRACTICE MAKES PERFECT. But he had marked it out in heavy ink, and substituted: SEE ME.

After class let out I stayed at my desk. He came around and sat on the edge of his.

I said, "My paper said to see you."

"Yes. You do not seem to be improving, so I think we should go back to an earlier exercise. Next time you come to class, I want you to type 'Now is the time for all good men to come to the aid of their country' over and over again until you can do it without really thinking about it. If you like, you can think of it as history—repeating itself."

I came to Mr. Farmer's next class with plenty of paper to do the exercise, but at the thought of the same sentence over and over and over, and nothing else in sight, I had to close my eyes.

". . . Number 22," intoned Mr. Farmer.

"Here," said Paul Vincent.

"Number 23."

"Here," answered Chelsea Wallace.

"Number 24."

"Here," I said.

And here I hang, self-crucified.

Oh, Lord, send your angels.

part *TWO*

The Book of LEE ANN

And he took up his parable, and said,
Balak the king of Moab hath brought me
from Aram, out of the mountains of the
east, saying, Come, curse me Jacob,
and come, defy Israel.
—*Numbers 23:7*

When I first got my car I had a little accident. Doesn't everybody? I don't think I ever met anybody who hasn't run into *something*. My fender bender happened on a rainy Tuesday on my way to school. My sister, Lee Ann, had missed the bus to middle school, so Mom made me drop her off on my way, and that made me late. There's this back road some of us use to get to school, so I turned onto it and was driving about forty miles an hour when I tried the one bad curve on the entire road.

It was the strangest feeling. I turned the wheel, but the car kept right on going. No screech of tires, no sensation of being slung to one side, just no control.

My car skidded off an embankment and plowed down a fence post before stopping. I wasn't hurt. No big deal.

It wouldn't have been anyway, except that there was plenty of other traffic, and at that moment a school bus full of little kids passed on its way to the elementary school.

A nice fat lady and her skinny husband pulled over and took me to their mobile home so I could call Dad to come get me. (Odd—Dad took care of the whole fence-post mess afterward, and I never really wondered about it until now. Did he pay off the farmer? How did I not end up with some kind of ticket? I suppose I'll never know; Dad doesn't answer a lot of questions.) The tow truck pulled my car back onto the road, and I got to school halfway into first period.

There's an experiment you can do with a large group of people where you have everybody sit in a circle and the first person whispers something in the second person's ear. That person whispers it to the next and so on until you've got all the way around the ring, and then the last person says aloud what the message was. The object is to see how much the news changed as it went around. You could start with something like "The blue penguin met the red pelican at the monkey cage" and end up with "The peacock ate the pink elephant."

Real news is like that too. When I got home after school, I found Mom in the kitchen giving Lee Ann a glass of milk and a Moon Pie. Mom is not a cookies-and-milk kind of mom, but Lee Ann had been crying.

"What happened?" I asked.

"See? He's all right," Mom said to my sister. "He's perfectly fine." Lee Ann stared.

"What's the matter, Mom?"

"She heard you had been killed in an accident."

"What!"

Lee Ann wiped her mouth. "Ellen Seal heard it from Kelly Parrish who was waiting for the bus at the elementary school and heard it from Matthew Chang's little sister who *saw* you wreck."

"When did you hear this?"

"This morning. Ellen came right in and told me."

"So you thought I was dead all day."

"It's not funny."

"Well, I've returned from the dead. Is that the last Moon Pie?"

Anyway, the grapevine grew only a little more slowly the day Ellis, Carrie, Jack, and Theresa were suspended. Only on the day after did Lee Ann seek me in my room after school. Her eyes were wide, and she crept in the door instead of barging in as usual.

"Bruce?" she said.

"What do you want?"

"Bruce . . . did you really get all those kids kicked out of school?"

"What do you mean, 'all those kids'?"

"All your friends."

I had fetched my mom's Bible and had it in front of me; I was trying to find some words to settle the ache I'd felt since the others left school. I'd been trying to find something in it that would say, "Yea, verily I say unto you, you did right, Bruce." But I just kept meeting up with rebuked pharisees.

I settled now for using the book as a shield to keep from meeting Lee Ann's eyes.

"Yes."

"Wow."

I peeked over the top of the book.

"I didn't know it would happen."

"You mean, it was sort of an accident?"

She wanted me to say so. I could hear it in the way she half whispered the question. I could see it in the way she clutched the hem of her shirt in her hands.

"No. It wasn't an accident."

"You mean you did it on purpose?"

"No! I didn't mean for it to happen the way it did. It just . . . happened."

"*What* happened?"

Sisters. Every guy in the world who has a sister knows how dangerous it is to tell her anything; a secret in a sister's ear is a weapon stockpiled for later use. But sometimes you can tell her things, and it helps. So I told Lee Ann what happened, and she didn't say anything for a long time. Then she said, softly, "I can't believe you did that," and went to her room. She shut the door and in a minute I heard Elvis Presley singing "You Ain't Nothing But a Hound Dog."

I didn't expect her to understand me. Lee Ann is worse than Mom about trying to make me "normal." Lately Lee Ann has been trying to get me to wear a baseball cap backward on my head.

The whole thing was so clear-cut to me I thought Jack and the others would see it too. I swear I did. And when I was surprised I expected them to see that also. When they didn't, I kept wanting to say, "No, wait, it's not like that at all!" but they didn't hear me anymore. A few days before, my friends could hear my voice. Now I might as well have been mute, and blind and deaf as well, because I was shut away from them, alone. There was no one to understand me, and I *wanted* someone. I'm beginning to think I don't even understand *myself*.

Mom had supper on the stove when I went downstairs. I lifted the pot lids with timid fingers, but there was no asparagus. I felt more steady.

"Hungry?" she asked, setting biscuits on the table.

"A little."

Dad looked up from where he was whipping potatoes.

"Strange. You've usually got a hollow leg."

Can there truly be so little rapport within a family? I like to imagine that some families enjoy a happy state in which parents and children can sense each other's moods and know when not to say certain things. Not so the Wells household.

I tried to picture saying at the dinner table, "Guess what I did in school this week. I got four of my friends suspended."

I could envision Dad with a forkful of potatoes stopped in midair; I could envision Mom shaking her head for two point five seconds and then saying, "Oh, Bruce! What do you mean?" In short, they would act the way they did the time I fought Roy Mullins in seventh grade for calling me a "pud" (I didn't know what this meant, and I'm sure Roy didn't, either, but whatever it was, I wasn't going to take it).

I came home with scrapes and bruises. Faced with a crisis, Mom can be very businesslike. With her mouth set in a tidy line, she cleaned and bandaged me, sat me at the table, and set my supper in front of me. But as she sank into her own seat her second nature took over, letting the fright and worry seep through her softening features.

"Oh, Bruce, what on earth?" she said, after her head stopped shaking.

I explained, and she let her food get cold thinking. Then she said, "Did you hurt the other boy?"

She didn't mean "Did you lick him"—she wanted to know if I had injured Roy Mullins. She already knew how badly I was hurt, and had treated me; now she could spare a thought for somebody else. The imagination I get from my mother made me see Roy with a sore, throbbing lip, and feel it too.

If Mom was Our Lady of Compassion, Dad was the patron saint of Reason. He of the holy eyebrow, which he raised.

"I'm sorry you felt you had to fight," he said. "Did you try reasoning with him first?"

"Dad, he called me a 'pud.' "

"So?"

Dad, with this one word and a twitch of his eyebrow, shifted the burden of proof onto me, and anything I could have said would have sounded mean and small. I don't play checkers with Dad anymore for the same reason; I never, ever win.

It was a double whammy—Mom made me *feel* and then feel guilty, and Dad showed with clinical efficiency how unnecessary the whole thing was, and suddenly I felt like I ought to apologize to the little scab.

I do it to myself now, and they've come to expect it of me; if I told them about the expulsions, their voices, like Lee Ann's, would plead, "*Say it isn't so. You're our Bruce, our wonderful child, our saint.*"

If I said, instead, "Mom, I'm sorry to tell you this, but I've murdered seven people and hidden their corpses in the crawl space underneath the house," I would not stir as much dismay.

They wouldn't *want* to believe something about me they didn't want to be true; that's Mom's problem with asparagus. When I proved I wasn't the way they wanted me to be, they would ask, "What did we do wrong?"

There would be no telling Mom and Dad.

Qualification: there would be no telling Mom and Dad if Lee Ann would keep her trap shut. I rummaged through my arsenal and remembered that Mom knew nothing about the book *Makeup Yourself Beautiful* hidden behind Lee Ann's dresser. Lee Ann yearns to wear makeup, but isn't allowed. Yes. That would do nicely.

How do *I* know about it? It's a matter of survival to know these things. Brothers and sisters have their own form of Mutually Assured Destruction.

I don't go to Sunday school much anymore, because nobody in our youth group is serious about learning anything. Poor Mr. Kyle has no control over the whispering, giggling, poking, and prodding, and can't get a word in. I tried going that Sunday, though, because every second thought going through my brain went something like *WHAT HAVE YOU DONE?* and I needed somewhere to turn.

Mr. Kyle opened his Bible to a place he'd marked, and said, "How many of you brought your Bibles today?"

Mine and Mr. Kyle's Bibles, it turned out, were the only ones in the room.

"Okay, maybe you can just listen then, and I'll read from mine. We're going to look at the Book of Numbers today. . . ."

I watched Pat Richson moisten his index finger with spit and insert it in Molly Archer's ear.

"Now, let's not have any more of that," said Mr. Kyle. "C'mon, gang, let's get serious."

Any time a Sunday school teacher says to a youth group, "C'mon, gang, let's get serious," it's an unmistakeable sign that it's time to lower the lifeboats. The ship is going down.

At last Mr. Kyle got some order, and tried to make headway. "Today we're looking at Numbers 22. This chapter is best known for the story about Balaam and his Ass. . . ."

Poor Mr. Kyle had no sense of danger; it was as though he was walking through a pit of cobras blindfolded. Mr. Kyle was a man of faith.

Pat Richson, though my age, was a child of three. "Hey, Mr. Kyle," he said, "was it a hairy Ass?"

I picked up my Bible and headed for the sanctuary.

Sanctuary—it's an interesting idea: a place of security and protection, a place of immunity from law. But your own mind can spoil any sense of peace you can have in such a place, and mine kept going back to Ellis and Jack and Carrie and Theresa. They would not graduate in May. Carrie might have been valedictorian.

If it hadn't been for me.

I had sat in a pew near the back, looking at the wooden cross suspended over the altar. I centered on that shape, willing Him to appear, so I could ask, so I could get it straight.

Hroooooonnnnnggggggg, hrummmmmmmmm, spake the organ. Mrs. Raye had slipped in and had begun limbering up her fingers for the service.

No answer, here or now.

After church Lee Ann came to my room again and sat, unbidden, on my bed. She had changed out of her Sunday best and now wore a black Motley Crüe T-shirt.

"You know what I think?" she said.

"Ah, that's a trick question, right? You don't think."

Her face pinched. "No, *really*. I think you should apologize. Not right now—wait until you see them again in school after Christmas. *Then* tell them you were wrong, and that you're sorry for what you did."

"You think I should apologize?"

"Yeah. It was your fault they were kicked out, and you should say you're sorry, at least."

"Wait a minute. I didn't do any kicking. Mrs. Atwell is the one who reported them. I didn't think she would do anything. If anybody got kicked in all this, it's me."

Lee Ann has one slim braid near her bangs, and she was forever twisting it. She twisted it now. "You *expect* teachers to do that. You don't expect your *friends* to sell you out. I mean, if you can't trust your friends, then who?"

Do you watch *Star Trek?* There's this episode in

which Captain Kirk and crew land on a planet where the humans are under the control of a computer named Landru. They're all wired into one mind, sort of, and they walk around saying, "Are you of The Body?" If Lee Ann, sitting there, had asked me, "Are you of The Body?" I wouldn't have been a bit surprised.

"Sis, I don't understand why you seem to think my reason for being on earth is to make myself just like everybody else. What if all my friends suddenly ran to the edge of a cliff and jumped off like a swarm of lemmings? Would you expect me to follow them? I'm not stupid. I think for myself."

Lee Ann got off my bed and crossed to the door. "Maybe you're not stupid," she said, "but that's a stupid excuse for getting four people kicked out of school." Then she went into her room and closed the door, and I heard the Beatles crank up with "I Want to Hold Your Hand." Lee Ann plays the Beatles when she wants to think about something else.

Now, I will tell you what was so strange about the way I felt talking to my sister, and thinking about my parents, and sitting in the church, questioning.

I felt scared. My hands went cold and my stomach soured whenever I thought about what I had caused. Ellis, Carrie, Jack, and Theresa—I was the cause of their pain. That made me afraid, for although I never rationally *thought* that I had done wrong, I began to *feel* that I had.

The Book of TROJANS

How shall I curse, whom God hath not cursed? or how shall I defy, whom the LORD *hath not defied?*
—Numbers 23:8

*E*ven if I could have forgotten about my four friends, it was not to be allowed. They had other friends besides me, and didn't someone once say, "The enemy of my friend is my enemy?" At least, that seems to be the code at Carthage North High School. I was the pariah. I was the leper. I was the wooden horse that hid the Greeks.

Soon after word got around, I went into lunch and found Sam Chapman, who I've known since sixth grade.

"Hi, Sam," I said. "Is anybody sitting here?"

"Uh—Bruce. Hey, yeah, I'm sorry. I'm saving that for Jennifer. She's in line getting her stuff. Sorry."

Four others were sitting at the table with him, and none of them spoke. But they all watched me as I turned away. Next I found an empty seat next to Marty Nichols at one of the long tables near the windows.

"Hey, Marty," I said, sitting.

He scooted his chair away a couple of inches. He was making room for me, I like to think. "Hi, Bruce," he muttered. I got settled and started to ask him how he did on the last physics test, but he suddenly waved at somebody across the room and stood up.

"Got to go," he said. "I promised Ronnie I'd sit with him and I just saw him over there. See you later, Bruce."

One by one, the chairs around me emptied the same way, until I sat alone. After three days of this, I stopped looking for anyone to eat with.

On the Tuesday before Thanksgiving, I was on my way to Latin during class change and I felt my foot catch on something. I fell, scattering my books, and then somebody's foot hit my ribs, hard, making me gasp and crunch my eyes shut.

"Sorry!" somebody said as he kept going down the hall. Two or three people giggled. I opened my eyes, but there was no way to tell who, in all that mob, had tripped me or kicked me. I gathered up my books— one had been kicked clear down the hall—but couldn't find my Latin notebook. A whole semester's worth of class notes, gone. And none of the people in the hall had seen, none of them had heard, none of them stopped to see if I was hurt.

If anyone was more despised than me, it was Mrs. Atwell.

Nobody talked much in her class anymore. Everybody gave cool, formal answers to her questions. Attendance at the Latin Club dwindled until Chuck Callis announced at one meeting that the meetings were canceled until further notice.

Students used to volunteer to help Mrs. Atwell carry her things to her car after school, but nobody did so now. One day she had a milk crate full of books to carry, and she hailed me going out the door.

"Bruce, could you come here a moment?"

I turned slowly, not really wanting to talk to her. "Yes, ma'am?"

"Bruce, could you help me get this crate out to my car? I've got an armload of other stuff to go, too, and I'd rather not make two trips."

I glanced at the door. "Actually, Mrs. Atwell, I do need to be going—"

"Oh, please, Bruce. You drive, don't you? It won't take a minute."

So I picked up the crate, waited as she turned out the light and locked the door, and then followed her down the (thankfully) empty hall. Then she surprised me.

"It's different without them, isn't it?" she said.

After I'd caught up with myself, I said, "Yes."

"It's a shame. Carrie and Ellis both are excellent students."

We walked farther down the hall, our footsteps clicking and echoing off the walls. Have you ever noticed how the walls in a high school seem jaded, like they've seen it all?

"When you asked me," I said, "I . . . I didn't know you were going to do anything."

"I'm glad you could tell me. I was so disappointed in those four. I thought I could trust them. I didn't want to have to report them at all, but it could have meant my job, and maybe Mrs. Tatum's, if word got out to parents. You know how news travels in this town."

Did I ever.

We exchanged not so much as a passing look before we arrived at the faculty parking lot in front of the building and I put the crate in her trunk. "Thank you, Bruce," she said. "I want you to know I'm glad I could trust you, at least." Then she put her hand on my shoulder. I didn't want it there; it meant we were alike, in cahoots, conspirators. *Et tu, Bruce?*

She got in her car and drove away.

I had begun to dread getting up for school each morning. One day Lee Ann sat down at the breakfast table and looked me over with a sister's suspicious eye.

"What's wrong with you, Bruce?" she asked.

"Nothing's wrong with me."

"You look like the living dead."

"Thanks ever so."

She leaned toward me and lowered her voice to an ineffective whisper. "It's what you did, isn't it? It's your guilty conscience."

"Eat your cereal," I said.

It wasn't my conscience, though that had been like a canker that hadn't given me any peace since it all started. It wasn't even the isolation at lunch, which I was getting used to. It was The Locker Room.

Jack had friends all over the school, and the more muscular of them were the lords of The Locker Room. Of these, Kurtis Dixon was chief banana, and he began a ritual with me every time we went to PE. "Hey, Wells," he would say, "catch!" Then he would hurl a medicine ball at me.

A medicine ball, in case you come from a more progressive school where medieval torture devices are no longer used, is an incredibly dense, heavy leather ball about the size of a soccer ball. Usually, one cannot throw such a ball very far, but Kurtis, bless him, can bench 225.

I'm a little nearsighted, and Kurtis knew I can't catch worth a damn. My skill in repelling all balls didn't help me, either, and every time, that medicine ball hit me with a solid, painful thump somewhere on my body. Ritual laughter followed from everybody who saw. Strangely, Coach Donne never witnessed it; or maybe not so strangely—Jack was one of Coach Donne's favorites.

Mr. Farmer said nothing else about the whole affair. He acted as though I were no different from anyone else, which, I think, was the hardest thing of all to take. Maybe that's why I went to see him over Christmas break.

Christmas is supposed to be a celebration of the coming of a savior to rescue Man from the results of his own actions. I had never appreciated a Christmas the way I appreciated this one—two and a half weeks of relief from the torment of school. But the same *inner* voice that spoiled my sanctuary in church wormed at me as the holiday drew closer. I needed answers.

On December 22 I went to Mr. Farmer's house. I knew where he lived because I had had to restrain Jack from toilet papering the trees in the front yard on Halloween. The only Christmas decoration visible from the outside now was a single red candle in the window standing in a circle of holly.

Mr. Farmer's car sat halfway in, halfway out of the carport, so I knew he was home. I rang the doorbell, and there was a long wait. Then the door opened, and there stood Mr. Farmer, wearing a plaid lounge jacket. I didn't know anybody wore those except in old movies.

"You're not the UPS man," he said. Then he looked

more closely and said, "Number 24?" I could see his surprise through the screen door.

"Yes, sir," I said, then added, "I am not a number."

"Yes. No. Well. What can I do for you, Mr. Wells?"

"I'd like to talk to you, if you have the time."

"Oh. Well, certainly."

We stood there for a few moments more, he expecting me to start talking, I suppose, and me expecting him to let me in.

"May I come in?" I asked, breaking the pause.

"Surely. Surely." He opened the screen door, and I got in out of the cold. He had a space heater going in his living room, next to a recliner. Books cluttered everything. There was no TV. Mom would never have let our house get so cluttered.

"Please, sit down," Mr. Farmer said, clearing a chair. I sat. He eased into his recliner, and said, "Now, what did you want to talk about? Grades have already been turned in to the main office, I'm afraid."

Have you ever noticed how you can always tell if somebody has a cat? Mr. Farmer's house smelled—no, stank—of cats.

"It isn't that," I said.

"No. I thought not."

A huge Persian cat appeared out of nowhere beside me on the couch. It put its forepaws on my leg and flexed its claws through my jeans. I unpicked them gingerly as I talked.

"Mr. Farmer, it sort of happened the way you said, and it sort of didn't."

He sniffed. "I must say I'm relieved I had no part in it."

"Do you think Mrs. Atwell should have turned them in?"

"That's hardly for me to say. One has to look after oneself. Mrs. Atwell had her job to think of. . . ."

I stroked the cat. Loose hair clung to my fingers. "I wonder if that's a good reason though."

Mr. Farmer raised his eyebrows. "A good *reason?* Mr. Wells, the very fact that you can ask me whether she *should* have turned them in tells me you believe she should *not,* and that her reason was not the right one. Let me ask you: should *you* have told *her?*"

I had to think. I should have known Mr. Farmer would get me over a barrel.

"More to the point, Mr. Wells, consider this: what if I *had* agreed to sponsor the five of you, and the same thing happened. Would you have told *me?*"

"I . . . I don't know."

He sighed and rubbed his forehead. "You vex me, Number 24. If you'd behave like every other adolescent at that school it would save trouble." He brought his palm down on his leg with a smack. "But you don't. Very well, I'll answer your question the best way I know how."

Another cat, a calico, leaped into his lap and curled

up, completely comfortable with the man; watching it only made me feel more uneasy.

"You want to know whether Mrs. Atwell was moral—no, scratch that, you want to know if *you* have a moral leg to stand on. Let's assume you acted morally. People are moral for four reasons: first, they fear punishment; second, they expect a reward; third, they believe they know what's best for others; and fourth, it is simply their nature to do so. As for the first two, they are rooted in selfishness—fear and desire. The third is based on conceit, which is insecurity, which comes back to fear, which returns to self. That leaves the fourth, the only one in which selfishness is not a factor. But this fourth one presupposes that you and I could even be able to take all the codes of conduct we've been taught since birth and winnow out of them an accurate sense of right.

"Now, I cannot read your mind, so I cannot tell which of the four is truest about you. But let us assume (to give you the benefit of the doubt) that you were motivated by the fourth, that you did what you did because it was your nature. What you don't understand is that nobody cares about absolutes. Absolutes have nothing to do with human lives.

"For the vast majority of people, conformity is the way to go—something I've tried to tell you over and over. Conformity is the balm that eases the contact between people and keeps down the pain, but true morality is a fly in that ointment—only *true* morality, that is, not the first three kinds. They can be understood for what they are, and dismissed. Mrs. Atwell acted for self-preservation. Not very noble, perhaps, but we can all see her reasons. The reason *you* have troubles—and I *have* noticed what's been going on—is that nobody really understands why you did it. So they substitute the reasons why they would have done it had they been in your position, and don't like what they see. It makes them dislike themselves."

My head spun. "So . . . I shouldn't have done it."

"I didn't say that. I only explain the results. I don't presume to judge you, except in the area of your typing ability. By the way, I notice that you registered for Typing II next semester."

"Yes. Don't I need it?"

"You do. You passed this semester, but only just." He left his chair and began straightening papers around the room. I got a feeling I should go.

"Thanks, Mr. Farmer," I said.

"Hm," he said.

I opened the door, but in my mind's eye I could see Mom telling me to be more mannerly than just walking out. I turned in the doorway and said, "Well, thanks again, and please tell Mrs. Farmer I said hello."

Mr. Farmer straightened and faced me slowly. He tilted his head and said, "Mrs. Farmer passed away many years ago, Mr. Wells. But your courtesy is noted."

"Oh. I'm sorry. . . . I . . . Merry Christmas. I mean . . . bye."

Idiot. Idiot. Idiot. Idiot. Idiot. No, Jack's the idiot, going on about Mr. Farmer and his wife. Jack's a fool. But I'm a worse one.

The Book of THERESA

For from the top of the rocks I see him,
and from the hills I behold him: lo, the
people shall dwell alone, and shall not
be reckoned among the nations.
—Numbers 23:9

Misery loves company.

The week before school started up again (on the obscenely early date of January 3) I was in town with Mom on the way to have my teeth cleaned and I saw them—The Four—walking together down the sidewalk, and something in me wanted to be with them. But I thought, they had probably spent the last few weeks together just so, and if together, then they must share the same feelings about me.

It's strange; Jack said I was the one who kept them together when they were the Disciples of Saint Bruce, and in a way it was still me keeping them together. Only they were against me now.

I imagined so, anyway, and the first day of school gave the proof.

In the cafeteria I had got my tray and was looking for some place away from other people to eat, when I saw them at the old round table. Theresa must have had a new schedule, because she was with them. The four of them stared at me. They didn't move, or speak; they stared. I turned away and tried to eat, but when I glanced back again, they still stared.

I couldn't stay. I dumped my half-finished lunch in the wastebasket and walked away.

In typing, the way things worked out, I was still Number 24. I said, "Here."

In Latin they were there, in their old seats. Mrs. Atwell had allowed them to register for this semester's class instead of retaking the last semester, but they were having to do extra work to catch up. I found a note on my desk, and opened it:

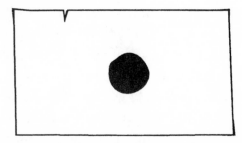

The Black Spot. That would have been Carrie's idea, á la *Treasure Island*. A rejection.

But they couldn't do it, not really. If they had pretended I didn't exist, *then* it would have been a rejection. But instead they stared, and left notes, and I thought, *They need me, still, for something.*

After the bell everybody made for the door, but I snagged Jack on the sleeve.

"Hi, Jack," I said.

He glared, jerked away, and left.

I think keeping up an intense grudge campaign must take such a tremendous amount of energy you can't keep it up for long. The Four kept up the stares and the spots for a couple of weeks, but then the spots stopped, and the stares began sputtering out too. Still, none of them spoke to me—except Jack.

Kurtis Dixon had stopped the medicine ball ritual as soon as Jack returned, but to my horror, Jack took it up. One day when I walked into The Locker Room, Jack stepped out from behind the lockers and said, "Hey, Bruce—catch!" and threw the medicine ball. Jack couldn't throw it like Kurtis (Jack could only bench 175, after all), but it was the principle of the thing. He *knew* about my eyes.

Ellis's revenge was far worse, because he held it back. He's a master at the mind game, and knowing that saved me a nervous breakdown. He would pass by me and chuckle softly, so I could hear. If I caught his eye, it was gazing at me clinically through narrowed eyelids.

He kept this up for days and days, and my imagination ran wild. I hardly dared open my locker, afraid of what might be in it.

But Ellis was never that crude or mechanical. His strike was more subtle, and he had nursed the plan a long time. Unlike Jack, who threw the medicine ball because it was the thing to do at the moment, Ellis plotted patiently for the long haul.

He even had accomplices who worked in his absence.

My lost Latin notes resurfaced the first week in February. I thought taking them had been some random maliciousness, but in fact it had been part of Ellis's scheme. I found the notebook on my desk when I came into Latin that first Friday, opened to a page in the middle.

How long Ellis had worked, I couldn't guess, but he had mimicked my handwriting and written:

Brad,
   I enjoyed the night we spent together and would like to do it again. You're really sexy. When would you be available? Let me know when and where. You know how I like it.

—Bruce

"Oh my God," I whispered, and shot my eyes around to Ellis, who smiled, very slightly. For an instant, I had a weird admiration—almost awe—for Ellis's genius. It *was* masterful. Given the generally accepted theory about Brad, nobody would question the note, and the handwriting was close enough to mine not to make anybody suspicious. Ellis gestured for me to turn the page, and I found, written in his own hand:

> *I thought you should have your notebook back. From what I hear it's been floating around all over the school.*
> *Cordially yours,*
> *Ellis*

After class ended, Ellis walked out with his head high, and the others followed, but Theresa hung back. I looked up at her, and she returned the look as though she wanted to say something. But it didn't come out, and she hurried after the others.

Have you ever read, and I mean *really* read, the tabloids at the supermarket? Jack used to buy the *National Enquirer* and the *Star* for laughs because they kept reporting about ninety-seven-year-old women having triplets and four-foot-long grasshoppers and men with horns growing out of their foreheads and kids raised by everything from bats to bears. Not everybody buys it to laugh at though. Our neighbor, Mrs. Banner, has stacks of them on her screened-in porch. You try your best to avoid her, but it's not always possible.

One day she spied me in the yard and said, "You'd better get in the house, young man!"

Alarms sounded in my brain, but in spite of them I said, "Why?"

"Sasquatch has been sighted just over the state line. You never know. You never do know." She brandished her copy of the *Enquirer* like a legal brief. "It says right here he snatched a child out of its cradle. The mother had only left it for a minute, and then Sasquatch had it."

I tried to tread carefully. "Mrs. Banner, I don't think there's anything to worry about. The stories in those papers aren't really true. . . ."

I had blasphemed. Mrs. Banner set her right hand on her hip and waved the paper with her left.

"That's gospel, that is," she said. "True as it can be. It's in black and white, and that makes it so."

Why are people so willing to believe the bizarre? Why are people so accepting of something scandalous, sordid, or strange? I don't understand it, but a good many at Carthage North High School were ready to believe the note Ellis planted. Jan Swenson is in her element spreading a good rumor. Whisper a little gossip and she's happy as Beulah the Cow. I don't suppose she's heard the one about her not wearing anything underneath, but as ye sow, so shall ye reap.

Jan swung into high gear with the note. Every time I walked down the hall a dozen pairs of eyes observed me, some with curiosity, some with loathing; I only had to swim up that current to find the source. I heard

Jan's voice in the Guidance Office as I passed, just as plain as you please—

"You mean you hadn't heard? Yes, Brad and Bruce are gay."

"You mean—?"

"I don't mean *happy*. They're gay *lovers*."

I stuck my head in the door.

"That isn't true," I said. "The note was a fake and it just isn't true."

The gossiper in this case was Melanie Spitzbergen, and she looked at me as though I were a Haitian zombie dripping gobbets of rotten flesh.

"Oh!" said Jan. ". . . Hi, Bruce. Look, Melanie, I've got to go. I'll talk to you later." She fled, disgustingly. Jan had none of Carrie's chutzpah; Carrie would have stood her ground like a cossack.

After that things slowed down, and I only heard about it from people I wouldn't have called friends anyway. But the damage was done.

The next week, after Kurtis Dixon had told me in the hall to "Get out of the way, fag" for the hundredth time, Theresa appeared next to me and said, "I wish Ellis hadn't done that."

"Oh. Hi, Theresa."

"Hi. Look, Bruce, I can't talk to you here, but I have some things I want to say. Are you free after school?"

"Yes. I guess."

"I'm going to Brookside Park to do my homework. I'll look for you by the lion drinking fountain. Okay?"

"Sure."

She went then, and I stood amazed. Theresa, of all of us, had had the nerve to cross the gap. I would have expected Jack or Carrie or even Ellis if he had thought he could belittle me, but not Theresa.

I went to the park, of course, as soon as school let out, and so I beat her there. Brookside Park's real name is Ann Frances's Brookside Park. It beats me who Ann Frances was, but the park has a great playground for the little kids, and there's a neat ride; it looks sort of like a shallow dish with two handles, and you lie down in it and turn around and around and around. It's been polished smooth by all the people who've ridden it over the years, people who liked watching the world move in unexpected ways. I lay on the metal made cold by the January air and turned. After a while I hung my head over the side, and Theresa's face flashed by three times before I could get stopped.

"You look silly," she said.

"Sorry. I was here early, but I was watching the fountain for you."

"It's okay. I saw you over here anyway. Let's go sit in the Pirate Ship."

The Pirate Ship wasn't really a ship, just a high raised platform with a ship's wheel and a pair of pretend spyglasses mounted on the rail. The ship overlooked the brook and the Wal-Mart beyond. She climbed the ladder into it and I followed.

"We made a pact not to talk to you," Theresa said on the top, leaning against the rail, "but I wanted to tell you a few things, so you'll know what you did." She looked out toward the store. "None of us will graduate in May, and I'll have to take summer school to be eligible for college this fall. So will Jack and Carrie." She looked back at me. "Carrie cried and cried."

My heart began a slow descent into my socks. Proud Carrie, crying.

"We were all really mad at first, but Ellis said getting mad was pointless, and that we should get even. Jack wanted to egg your house, but Ellis didn't like that either." She paused. "Ellis won't tell any of us what his folks did when they heard. I've heard his father has a bad temper."

Back to me, every time. Back to me.

"Jack and Carrie are grounded until the end of the school year—no parties, no movies, nothing. I got off easy because I've never been in trouble before." She suddenly twisted around and stared me square in the face. I had never seen her look so centered; Theresa, the scattered one. She said, "Will you just tell me why?"

I took a breath, and said what I had decided to say.

"Because she asked me."

"Did you even think about what would happen to us?"

"I didn't think she'd do anything."

"Well, she did."

"Theresa, I was as surprised as you were. She just said she needed to know."

"Then, you're sorry you told her."

My tongue started, but my brain checked it. "Do you mean," I said cautiously, "am I sorry I told her or am I sorry for what happened?"

"I mean, do you apologize for doing it?"

A biting breeze began blowing, whipping her red hair around her face, but she didn't move.

"I don't think I know," I said. Her eyes squinted, and she peered at me a minute before pulling her coat around her and turning away.

"I have to go," she said. "We can talk some more later."

She climbed down the ladder and jogged away toward the parking lot, leaving me on the Pirate Ship. I started shaking, not from the cold. I don't like confrontations. I started down the ladder to escape the cold, and I thought, *Theresa doesn't either. How strange. This wasn't her style at all. . . .*

The Book of PAMELA

*Who can count the dust of Jacob, and
the number of the fourth part of Israel?
Let me die the death of the righteous,
and let my last end be like his!*
—Numbers 23:10

"Give me a C!"

"C!"

"Give me an A!"

"A!"

Whatever the crowd might have been giving Ruth Hightower, it was giving me a headache. A new semester, a new season, and a new sport—basketball—had come, and our skilled, swift, and sturdy Carthage North High School Trojans needed a shot in the arm. The serum: pep rallies, as prescribed by Principal Tatum, specialist in sports medicine. I could imagine her sitting in front of her television with a beer in one hand and a bag of pretzels in the other, complaining at her husband running the vacuum in the other room.

After the suspension of the Latin Four, no clemency from pep rallies would be forthcoming for the next two centuries or so. Mrs. Tatum did not use those words, but they capture the essence. Mr. Farmer suffered now in silence; Mrs. Atwell stood by the doors with her fingers demurely in her ears; and Ellis, Carrie, Jack, and Theresa sat across the gym on the other bleachers in a solid, silent block. None of the cheerleaders cavorted in front of them, trying to get them to cheer because everybody knew better. But nobody knew the way *we* knew—them, Mrs. Atwell, and me. They knew, and knew I knew, and knew that I knew that they knew I knew, and Mrs. Atwell knew we knew, and the knowing ran between us like an electric current. But what I was *not* sure of was: did Mrs. Atwell really *know?* Did she understand? Did the current run through her the way it ran through me?

On Monday in Latin I watched her in front of the room, teaching the way she had taught ever since I'd been her student. Her face suggested no remorse or sorrow, or even that her mind had entertained a second thought about what had happened. I had to ask a question, before I could answer it myself.

When class ended, Ellis and Carrie jetted out; Theresa acted like she wanted to say something, but Jack paused too, and she hurried out with the first two. Jack looked from me to Mrs. Atwell a few times, but when I showed no signs of leaving, he left. Then it was only me and her, she cleaning the chalkboard and me at my desk.

"Mrs. Atwell, do you have a minute?"

"Bruce! Still here? Sure. What's up?"

I despise the phrase "What's up?" I think it should be reserved for the exclusive use of philosophers discussing the metaphysical relativity of spacial orientation, and not allowed for the average person who hopes to lighten what she knows is going to be a heavy talk. I got right down to it.

"I wanted to ask you a question about what happened with Ellis and Carrie and the others."

She sighed, and sat on the edge of her desk. Her hands began to look for something to do. "Okay," she said. "Shoot."

"Shoot" is another one of those phrases, but never mind.

"Are you sorry you turned them in?"

"No," she said, quick with the answer. "I'm sorry I had to, very sorry, but I didn't really have a choice."

"Did you even think about what would happen to them?"

"Of course I did. Well, some. I knew they would be disciplined. I thought suspension might have been a little extreme. . . ."

"Did you think," I said, and I felt a little quiver somewhere around my sternum, "about what it would do to me?"

She blinked. "What do you mean?"

"Before you did it, did you think about what would happen to me, or how I would feel?" I saw her pulling back, but I had to hear the answer.

"In all honesty, Bruce, no I didn't. It didn't really concern you."

"Were you just using me because you knew I'd tell you? Did you have no idea how people would look at me when it happened? You asked me, and I told you in confidence!"

"Bruce," she said evenly. "You didn't ask me to keep it secret. I asked you for the information because I knew you would be honest about it if you knew, but I didn't *force* you to tell me. And you can't blame me for using it the way I had to."

From that moment I ceased to blame Pamela Atwell. I understood her *reasoning* perfectly, and realized that her reasons were not my reasons.

I was glad I had asked her, because her answer left me ready for what happened next. When I left her room and went to my locker I found Jack standing there with his arms crossed over his chest. Jack's an open person—he never holds people at arm's length, but now he had a beware-of-dog look.

"Hey, Jack."

"Hey. What's going on?"

"Nothing much." I looked down the hall both ways. "Should you be talking to me? Theresa said Ellis—"

"I'm not Ellis's pet rock. And I want you to know I had no part of that note. I mean, you had something coming, but that note was low. I've been telling everybody it isn't true."

"Thanks. Listen," I said, "did you get in much trouble?"

"Me? Nah, Dad thought they were crazy. He wanted to raise Cain, but Mom said it wouldn't make any difference. It tore Carrie up awful bad, though, and Theresa."

"What about Ellis?"

Jack had unfolded his arms, and slouched his full weight against the lockers, more like the usual Jack LaRue. "He won't say. But I've heard his dad's a bastard. I reckon he got thrashed or something."

"No! Surely . . ."

Jack shrugged. "You're the one who opened the can of worms."

"Jack—"

"I know, you didn't want to know about the whiskey to start with. I'm still figuring you out, Bruce, who you are and who you aren't, what you do and what you don't. What makes you different."

I got my things stowed in my locker and closed the door. "I haven't figured it all out yet myself. I'm still trying to figure out what needs to be figured out."

"Then maybe you'll learn something when we have it out."

"What do you mean?"

He said, "You'll see. Talk to you later." Then he jogged off down the hall toward the front doors.

I thought maybe the ice had begun to thaw, but the next day at lunch the four of them sat together and stared at me until I couldn't eat. I thought about going to their table, though Ellis daunted me; he had dressed in black—shirt, pants, and mood. But his looks made me wonder more and more what he thought, until my curiosity overcame my good sense. I left my tray where it was.

Their eyes followed me like tracking radar as I walked up to their table and said, "Hey." Ellis disemboweled me with eye daggers of Toledo steel (only the best for Ellis).

"Hey," said Jack, but he dared go no further with Ellis so murderous. Theresa said nothing, just sat there with her hands in her lap. Carrie surveyed me coolly, and then said, "You have been excommunicated. Go away."

I went. But right before Latin, Theresa caught my sleeve near the guys' rest room and said, "Can you come to the park again today?"

"I can't today. My sister is staying late for band practice at the middle school and I have to pick her up."

"Tomorrow, then?"

"Okay."

"In the Pirate Ship this time. You will come?"

"Yeah. Sure."

"Good. See you."

In Latin she behaved as though nothing had passed between us.

Did I tell you Lee Ann plays the clarinet? Maybe I didn't. She doesn't play it very well, so I try to blot it out of my mind. Lee Ann has a long history of hobbies that make a racket. The last thing she was into was tap dancing. I nearly lost my mind.

When I went into the middle school to pick her up, I found her sucking on her reed as though it was an extension of her thumb.

"I *don't* suck my thumb," she said, when I told her. "*I'm* not insecure."

I got in the car and unlocked her side. "What do you mean by that? Are you saying I am?"

She opened the passenger door and got in. "*May*be, maybe *not,*" she replied in a singsong, juvenile, nanny-nanny-boo-boo kind of way. You can rely on your sister to *be* your sister no matter what.

"Don't be stupid. What are you saying?"

"You just are, the way you try to be what everybody wants you to be."

"Well, where did you get all that? I know you didn't come up with it yourself."

"Stephanie Hightower said your friends called you Saint Bruce."

I pulled out onto the main highway and headed home. "They don't anymore."

"No, duh. Anyway, you never were one. I know what you keep hidden in your room."

"Shut up." She has an uncanny way of unnerving me with that—of making my mind run paranoid circles trying to think what she could conceivably have found. I shook it off and said, "Do you listen to everything Stephanie Hightower says?"

"She heard that from her sister, but no, I don't. I had to mash her in the mouth when she said it."

"Lee Ann!"

"I'm kind of sorry now, because I think she might be right, but she was talking about my family, and that's good for a mouth mashing."

After a minute I asked, "Did she bleed?"

"Not much. I took it easy on her. But she was right, because you let them call you a saint when you're not one. Why *did* you?"

I drove past the Winn-Dixie, the lawn and garden place, and the Third National Bank before I could even say, "I don't know . . . exactly."

"See?" said Lee Ann. "Insecure."

The next afternoon I drove to Brookside Park after school. I looked across the playground at the Pirate Ship, but I couldn't see Theresa. She'd passed me a questioning look in Latin and we'd exchanged nods, so I knew she was coming. I took a drink at the lion fountain and wandered around, waiting. After a while, the cold began to seep through my coat, so I decided to climb into the ship, where the rails would block the wind. I pulled myself quickly up the ladder, but stopped short with my head just above floor level. Sitting there, huddled shoulder to shoulder, were Theresa, Jack, and Carrie.

"Idiot," said Carrie, untangling herself from the other two. "Wandering around out there like a lost sheep."

"Sorry. I—didn't know you were here."

"Obviously."

"You could have called out."

"No. We have to keep some decorum in these proceedings."

"What proceedings?"

"This," Carrie said, "is an Inquisition."

The Book of CARRIE

And Balak said unto Balaam, What hast thou done unto me? I took thee to curse mine enemies, and, behold, thou hast blessed them altogether.
—Numbers 23:11

Have you ever wondered why more people you know don't become famous? I've met several people here at Carthage North High School so full of skill and ability you'd think they were headed straight for the big leagues. Take Rupe Lawson. He was a senior when I was a freshman, and I saw him play on the basketball team. To me, basketball is usually about as exciting as watching the toilet flush, but Rupe's playing was different. He had smoothness. He had grace. He had a single-mindedness with the game that made it hard sometimes to tell where the ball ended and Rupe began. Rupe had star quality.

Rupe Lawson is now the cashier at the Minit-Mart on the corner of Caldwell and Main.

Or take Evelyn Moore; half the debate trophies in the school's glass display case were Evelyn's conquests for the greater glory of Carthage North High. She had a mind like a wild cat's—always alert, always aware, always in control and ready to spring. Everybody said Evelyn was going to go to an expensive private college and then blow them all away at law school. She could have too.

But Evelyn Moore was sent to Lakeland Rehab Hospital for a drug habit.

What causes people you know to fall short of themselves—or short of the expectations you have for them? I once thought it was just lack of opportunity, like with Rupe. Then I thought perhaps it was because the people had flaws that brought them down. Later I thought it might just be destiny getting in the way—people becoming what they were meant to become instead of something else. Now I think it's probably (d) all of the above. Or at least some of the above.

I wonder about Carrie. Carrie's quick and running over with imagination, and always, always theatrical. I think she could be a famous actress someday, or a writer. But you never know what's going to happen. What possessed her to drink Ellis's whiskey? What if she tries to get a job someday, or go to college, and somebody looks at her record and says, "Hm, I see you were suspended from high school. Too bad, we could have used you."? Will it be her fault for having drunk the Jack Daniel's, or my fault for having told, or is it just that we were fated to do what we did because of who we are?

I don't know.

Maybe nothing like that will happen. Maybe she won't *let* anything get in her way. Maybe she'll be the one of all of us who does the great thing that makes her famous. She certainly kept in practice.

"Climb in," she demanded imperiously, gesturing for me to sit against the opposite rail.

"What do you all want?" I asked, sinking down. The wind snuck in between the rails, but the others didn't show that they felt it.

"I said this is an Inquisition. This is a tribunal for disclosure and punishment. We three are your jury, and you are to stand trial for what you have done."

I pulled my coat tighter around me. There we sat in a kids' playground, and if we had been little kids, what Carrie was doing would have been called playing. But Carrie wasn't pretending. Jack shifted around, uncomfortable; this wasn't his style any more than bringing me to the park the first time had been Theresa's. All became clear—Carrie had set them to it from the start. Carrie was the one acting without Ellis.

"Where is Ellis?" I said.

Carrie took an envelope from an inside pocket of her coat and removed the contents: a roll of paper. "Ellis is not part of these proceedings." She unrolled the scroll of paper, and I could see through it by the sunlight filtering through the rails. Carrie had used calligraphy to write on it. This was every bit as elaborate as Ellis's note in my notebook. "Shall we begin?" she said.

Theresa and Jack each nodded as Carrie looked at them in turn. Then she held up the scroll and began reading in a precise, firm voice.

"These are the charges that face the Accused, Bruce of Carthage, for acts which he did perpetrate against four persons of his acquaintance"—she gave *acquaintance* a bitter stress—"in the fall of the year previous: that he, one, impersonated and pretended to be a saint with all the personal qualities pertaining thereunto; that he, two, divulged confidences placed with him by persons of his *acquaintance* whom he had led to believe in his sainthood; and that he, three, caused grievous harm to these persons by divulging said confidences." She rolled up the scroll. "Do you have anything to say before we present the case?"

Before the pep rally campaign, if Carrie had talked us into doing something like this, Jack would have been squirming like live bait and Theresa would have had an unquashable fit of giggles. Now, even if this wasn't Jack's way, and even if Theresa could see the funny side of it (I couldn't), their faces were stone.

I shook my head.

"All right, then," said Carrie. "We will begin with the first charge, that you impersonated a saint. Jack, will you tell us, please, why you thought of the accused as 'Saint' Bruce?"

Jack, who had been sitting Indian style, unfolded and raised both his knees to his chest, wrapping his arms around them. "I called him Saint Bruce because I never met anybody so perfect. Or anyway, anybody who tried to be so perfect. I never met such a straight arrow. I mean, he doesn't smoke or spit on the floor or cuss or fool around or fight or lie, or any of the other stupid crap the rest of us do. And he gets good grades and the teachers like him. Most everybody does—or did."

"Thank you, Jack. Theresa?"

Theresa wove her fingers together and studied her shoes. "I guess it's the same with me as with Jack," she said. "And he always listened if I had something to say, unlike some people."

There was a brief, tense pause, then Carrie gathered herself and went on. "All right. For my part, Bruce, I thought you were above the common mass of people because you actually thought before you said or did anything, and I never saw you do a single wrong thing, so I was fooled along with the rest. I trusted you just like the others when we told you about that Friday; we figured, oh, Bruce is a saint, he won't tell anybody. Bruce is cool. Bruce is hip. Bruce can be trusted. But now we know you couldn't be. Now we know."

"Next charge," she said, shifting gears. "What you were told you were told in confidence, and I think you knew it. Wouldn't you agree that that was pretty clear at the time, Jack?"

Jack looked like it was all leaving him behind. "I guess so. Yeah."

"Theresa?"

"I didn't think he would say anything."

"Exactly. We trusted in the goodness he claimed to have. Yet knowing that the information was secret, he told Mrs. Atwell, with the most *unfortunate* results. This brings us to the third charge, that the accused caused grievous harm to his acquaintances. The truth of this is unquestionable. Jack, tell the court what happened to you after the accused divulged our confidences."

"Carrie, can't you just speak English?" Jack said, but he shrank under her glare, sighed, and did his part. "Dad hit the stratosphere when I told him I got kicked out, but he's all smoke and no bang, so I just got grounded for the rest of the year. He was more mad at Mrs. Tatum for telling him he should set a better example in the home."

"The point being," Carrie interposed, "that you have lost your liberty for months. As," she added, "have I. It nearly killed my parents that their daughter got thrown out of school."

Theresa said, "I already told you I got off easy. My folks said having to go to summer school ought to be punishment enough, but they were mortified."

"You make ripples," Carrie said, pointing at me. "You didn't just hurt us, you hurt the people around us. Did you rat on us because you wanted Brownie points with Mrs. Atwell? Or are you just basically low in character? What have you got to say?"

"It sounds," I said after a moment, "like I'm already convicted."

"Maybe you are. Remember, I said we're your jury. Not your judge. We leave the judgment to you. Judge yourself guilty or not, and declare it now."

She said no more, and the three of them waited. The three of them, already convicted and punished, subjected to justice, but not mercy, condemned not by Pamela Atwood, but by me. And now they sat there, offering me the mercy of self judgment. Carrie sniffed and tilted her head slightly, expectantly, questioning.

"What I wonder," I said, "is why you four were so willing to think I was so perfect to start with. I didn't pretend to be *anything*. You're the ones who came up with it. You're the ones who took that drink. Jack told me you wanted me around, that you needed me. Is that what this is about now? Do you need me to be guilty? I *am* guilty. I did it. I told. Now I wish I hadn't—not because *you* don't *approve*—but because *I'm* not sure what's right anymore."

I wiped my clammy, sweaty palms against my jeans, then stuck them in my coat pockets to get warm. None of the others spoke, and nothing they did gave much clue to their thoughts. Only Jack's fidgeting told me he wanted to be elsewhere. At length Carrie arched an eyebrow and looked at the rolled-up scroll on her lap.

"Does that," she said, "conclude the case for the defense?"

"Yes."

"Then this Inquisition is finished. We will assess punishment and advise you in due course."

She looked a little funny there, half blue with the chill, trying to be magisterial, but she gamely kept it up as she went to the ladder and climbed down. She could do nothing else, except react within the limits nature had set on being Carrie.

Theresa followed her, almost helplessly. Theresa always bent to a stronger will than her own, and always would; that was *her* nature. Jack, though, stopped and faced me before going down the ladder. I had known his features for years, and had only lately found them unreadable. But now I saw something—something more familiar, if only very slightly.

"Look, maybe we all . . . ," he began, then broke off and finished with, "See you tomorrow."

I collapsed when I got home, weak and tired, and glad, glad, glad that Mom had supper almost ready. Aromas of roast beef and sweet potatoes salved me as I lay on the couch. Mom called from the kitchen, "Bruce, you eat asparagus, don't you?"

I sighed and sat up. There are some struggles, I realized, you never completely win.

The Book of NUMBERS

And he answered and said, Must I not take heed to speak that which the LORD hath put in my mouth?
—Numbers 23:12

What's the deal with convertibles? Why is it everybody admires a vehicle that looks like a normal car that's been driven underneath a low limb at high speed? I can't figure out the appeal. I rode in my cousin's convertible once and she kept on and on about how she loved to feel the wind in her hair and see the sky spreading open all around her. She had to shout her tonsils out to say it because her radio's volume shook nearby buildings, and the engine and the wind combined to drown out everything the radio missed.

Unlike my cousin, I didn't like the sky spreading. I don't suffer from agoraphobia or anything, but I constantly felt like the hand of God was coming down to squash me like a flea. Thou shalt not tempt the Lord thy God, and driving around in a car with no lid seems to me to tempt.

I don't think my cousin told me the truth though. I'm not even sure she realized why she really loved the car, but it was plain to me. At every third stoplight some guy would honk, or, if he had his window open, would say something like "Kickin'!" My cousin would flirt disgustingly. She liked her convertible, clearly, because it got her noticed, the hand of God notwithstanding.

Convertibles make a perfect example of the great paradox of everybody wanting the same thing because owning it will make them recognized as individuals. But think: what if *everybody* owned a convertible? Suddenly no one would be any different from anybody else. What would happen? Convertibles would have all the social collateral of a toothbrush, and everyone would go slavering after something else.

I only mention convertibles because I once heard Ellis laugh in scorn at Kurtis Dixon (behind his back, of course; the debate still goes on over whether Kurtis would have pummeled him or whether Ellis could have fended Kurtis off by sheer force of personality, but Ellis was never interested in dangerous gambles) when Kurtis bragged that he would be getting a convertible for his birthday. Kurtis didn't realize that the social benefits of ownership only last if the car actually appears, and as his convertible was as mythical as most (if not all) of his sexual conquests beneath the bleachers, Ellis made much hay out of it. Finding Kurtis in the hall, he'd say, "So, Kurt, how's your ride? Still purring like a kitten?"

Ellis did that because he could, to satisfy his mean streak. But I think he started on me in the days after the Inquisition for another reason.

"So, Bruce," he said to me on Thursday, "how's your love life?"

It startled me that he had spoken at all, after the arctic silence I'd grown used to.

I said, "That was deep-down rotten, Ellis."

"You would know," he replied. "You're a specialist in deep-down rotten."

Another surprise. Ellis does not resort to "takes one to know one"; he doesn't need to. So why now?

Later he found me outside the gym and said, "Going to PE, Bruce? Does it turn you on watching the guys dress out?"

"It's gotten old, Ellis. Jack's already told most people it isn't true, so why don't you just drop it?"

I've seen people's faces turn white or very red or even slightly purple, but I swear Ellis's face turned gray. The hall around the gym is kind of dark—maybe the shadows in that dark hall had something to do with it. His head sunk between his shoulders, and though his eyes had narrowed, they seemed even more white.

"Jack is a fool," said Ellis. "So is Theresa, and Carrie's blind. They don't see you the way I see you.

You're a whited sepulchre. I don't know what sadistic pleasure you got out of screwing us, but I hope it was worth it. Because of you I won't be going to college for two, three years at least. My father said, 'If you have nothing better to do in school than swill down the sauce, then I'm not paying for you to go.' I'll have to work and save money on my own now."

This wasn't a formidable Ellis; I hardly knew this person. But then, I hardly knew him to start with.

"Ellis," I said, "there are scholarships—"

"You disgust me. My parents were *proud* of me, but that changed, because of you."

"Jack said . . . I mean, did your dad—"

"My dad," he said hoarsely, "is none of your business, *Saint* Bruce."

He turned away and stalked down the hall, slightly bent, like someone carrying something heavy on his back.

On the first day after Carrie's Inquisition, she and the other three still sat at their table in the cafeteria, and Ellis stared, but the others didn't. On the second day they had an argument. I couldn't hear what it was about.

Then the third day came, and my luck ran better than usual because I nabbed a round table in the corner by the windows just before another guy got there. I liked a small table because I didn't have to worry about people getting up and leaving. The Four sat, as always, at their table, but they weren't in my line of vision and they couldn't stare, so I took more interest in my lunch.

A smacking sound crossed the room—a book against a table. We all looked up like a field of prairie dogs, and I watched Carrie, Jack, and Theresa stand, gather their things, and leave Ellis sitting at his table.

They came to mine, set down their trays, pulled out chairs, and sat. Carrie gave the table a single rap with the butt of her knife and directed the rounded point at me.

"Hear the ruling of the Tribunal," she said. "We have found you, Bruce of Carthage, guilty as charged of impersonating a saint and of betraying your friends. Your admission of guilt weighed in your favor, however, and the members of the Tribunal are willing," she said, with a sidelong glance at Jack, "to accept a certain amount of responsibility for their own actions. The Tribunal has decided that, barring any repeat offense, your sentence is commuted.

"But nothing is forgotten," she added. "Nothing. Do you understand?"

I nodded.

"And you will never be called 'saint' anything ever again. You are not worthy of any such title, as you proved when you spilled your guts to Mrs. Atwell. Clear?"

"Yes."

"Just so you understand."

• • •

I can now number my friends three greater than I believed I could only weeks ago, and if there's still a distance between us, at least the ache of isolation is gone. Anything but that. Almost anything.

Looked at the other way, I guess I have to number them one less. I don't suppose Ellis spoke to any of us the rest of the year. I don't know who else he would have spoken to—he didn't have many friends. I think Jack tried to draw him out a couple of times, but Jack doesn't beat dead horses, and he finally gave up on Ellis.

None of them was ever more than civil to Mrs. Atwell, either, but if it bothered her (and I think it must have) she never let it show. I can't criticize them, because I, myself, never let her get as close to me as she had been. Some bonds, once broken, just don't mend whole.

"Number 22," intoned Mr. Farmer in typing the next day.

"Here," said Scott Underwood.

"Number 23."

"Here," answered Holly Weldon.

"Number 24."

He wanted me to say "here," to slip into the mold, snug and comfortable as a foot in a warm sock. I watched him, but he kept his eyes on his roll book.

"Number 24," he repeated.

"I am not a number," I said. "I am a free man."

He looked at me over his bifocals and breathed a short sigh. "I will take that to mean," he replied, "that you are here."